D1301830

SECRET DESIRES –
Two Erotic Romances

First Magic Carpet Books, Inc. edition September 2005

Published in 2005

Manufactured in the United States of America
Published by Magic Carpet Books, Inc.

Magic Carpet Books, Inc.
PO Box 473
New Milford, CT 06776

Library of Congress Cataloging in Publication Date

Secret Desires - Two Erotic Romances
Digging Up Destiny by Frances LaGatta
Dreams & Desires by Laura Muir
$12.95

ISBN# 0-9766510-7-6
Book Design: P. Ruggieri

TABLE of CONTENTS

Digging Up Destiny

Frances LaGatta

To Laura Gatta, the best friend and mother a daughter could ever hope to have. Web publisher Bethany Burke, who opened doors in both careers and went the extra mile besides. And, Missa Mia, who without her love and support my destiny would not be realized.

Chapter One

Archeologist Blake Sevenson ignored the mosquitoes feasting on his mud-baked neck and continued to shovel madly. He stood, seemingly buried in a self-made grave, digging away at a Peruvian mountainside where the jungle canopy gave way to higher altitudes. This largely unexplored eastern slope, edged by Amazonian rainforest, was aptly called the *cejas de la selva*, or the 'eyebrows of the jungle'.

Cocking his brow, Blake could see why the Incas believed gold was the tears shed by the sun; shafts of sunlight streamed through the treetops, transforming recent raindrops into golden tears that glistened on the greenery. If the Incas thought gold was also the sweat shed by the sun, he was tired of sweating nuggets for naught in blasted weather more unpredictable than a woman.

Ready to call it a day, he speared his shovel into the sodden mound before him. The vibrating oak handle reminded him of a colossal finger flip-off. Narrowing his eyes, he visualized a one-armed bandit on a slot machine. With a two-fisted grip and a strained grunt, he let loose a war cry and forced the handle down. Multicolored parrots squawked in fright and scattered from peaceful perches in a rain of wet leaves. Blake's voice mocked him, echoing loudly throughout the Cordillera. Bent over, as if bowing low before the *Apus*, the 'mountain spirits' of the Incas answered his demand for pay dirt.

The whole hillside gave way, slopping mud over his head. It traversed his naked shoulders and back in a sickening slide. He struggled to straighten up, cringing as the heavy burden on his back oozed off into the seat of his jeans. He skimmed muck from his face. Brown blobs dropped from his hair to bomb his chest. Opening a wary eye, he glanced down to where his legs and boots had been before he gambled on *Pachamama*. 'Mother Earth' had not been kind. He would have to sling mud faster than a politician to dig himself out, much less clean up his act. At any rate, he would never make it in time to meet Hope Burnsmyre at the summit of Machu Picchu.

If only something as simple as a shovel could dig him out of that mess. University grants and private donations for his expeditions were a godsend. Yet recent monies provided by the Winslow Foundation had come along with a contingency clause he could live without: specifically one Hope Burnsmyre. According to her résumé and the Foundation's reports, she was single, twenty five years young, and quite ambitious. She'd come to him armed with a brand spanking new PhD from Stanford and, no doubt, high hopes for him as her mentor. She needed field work hours and would learn at his knee while doing her post doctorate in cultural anthropology. More or less independent, she would definitely be too attached to him for his comfort. Basically, she'd be chained to his hip while serving out an entirely too long one year sentence with him as her master. And in short, if he didn't baby sit, he wouldn't get paid.

Blake slung another shovelful of muck over his shoulder. While he didn't need the inconveniences Ms. Burnsmyre would propose, she certainly needed his autograph added to her impressive résumé along with a cultural observation of the natives. Nevertheless, if she couldn't befriend his locally hired farmers – she'd never make the grade. He couldn't make the *campesinos* accept her. She had to earn their trust and respect. And that was no easy assignment. These highlanders, who were direct descendants of the Incas, shunned their own modernized people who eroded their ancient beliefs and traditions. They looked upon outsiders with less than, well, she would hardly approve of them peeing downwind on a dig, but an all male to a one female archeology team was the least of his worries. While Ms. Hope-of-High-Hopes was familiar with a few words, she couldn't speak the native Quechua language, and he had neither the time to act as her translator, nor the inclination to mollycoddle this unwanted protégé.

Blake visualized a horse-faced fusspot who would quote from her textbooks like a televangelist. A Sherman Tank who would probably try to roll over him, create chaos, hand him a long list of special dietary needs – 'requirements' that would inspire hypochondriacs to compose songs in her honor. He pulled his left leg from the quagmire and an uncouth suction sound mocked him.

Even worse, he'd stubbornly put off all but the basics of her impending arrival to the point where essential concerns were too late. Like the fact that jetlag and mountain climbing didn't mix. Her thirteen-hour flight to Cuzco, followed by a ride on a rickety train to the mountain base, was not the best precondition for hiking the Inca trial to the summit of Machu Picchu. Peering down sheer rock faces that reduced the roaring Urubamba River into a white rope had made his own head lasso with vertigo. And whatever possessed him to send Pedro as her guide? His body odor alone could kill flies – unless they got close enough to bite him and died from alcohol poisoning. So, maybe Pedro wasn't the best example of Peruvian hospitality, but an anthropologist should know that North and South were planets apart when it came to life and living in the Americas.

Then again, Ms. Burnsmyre may never make it to the train station. She could come down with altitude sickness. Not that he'd ever wish it on a soul. It had taken him two days of bed rest before he acclimatized. Yet, his journey to the Lost City in the Clouds had been worth every ailment, blister, scrape, and near slip into oblivion. The breathtaking vistas made him wonder how anyone could question the existence of a divine creator. When he had unhooked his backpack at the Gateway to the Sun, time itself held its breath, and the unanswered mysteries of the ruins revitalized his need to unearth.

After three years of simpler living among the Quechua natives, he decided to hang his hat here for good and never look back. Trouble was, Hope Burnsmyre reminded him too much of the life he had left behind. He had once hoped for an assistant who would be willing to risk dysentery in a third world country, and just for the chance to piece together potsherds that may or may not answer an unsolved puzzle of the past. He had interviewed too many starry-eyed student treasure seekers over the years and dropped his professorship as a result. A few qualified females had gone as far as to offer him sexual favors for a chance to break into archaeology. The males were as bad with their Indiana Jones philosophies: not a dedicated historian in the bunch. They had no idea that the chance of discovering a tomb that had not been robbed was about a million to one.

Blake rammed his shovel into the maddening mud and a metallic clang jolted his wrists and spine. His heart stopped. Adrenaline pumped through his bloodstream. His men's constant chatter roared in his head; Inca gold secreted in these mountains during the Spanish siege. Muck oozed between his frantic fingers as his hand, forearm, and elbow disappeared, sinking clear up to his shoulder. Cheek pressed to the mud, his searching fingers made definite contact with a smooth and embossed object the size of a dinner plate. His hand swept madly about facial features surrounded by sunrays.

Tearing out mud like a dog to a bone, he at last saw the undeniable gleam of a pure gold. "*Inti*," Blake breathed the name of the Inca sun god.

Locals believed this golden relic marked the hiding place of Atahualpa's lost ransom. Legend had it that this last ruling Inca king's spirit guarded the entrance to subterranean tunnels and caves housing the last of the 'sweat of the sun' and 'tears of the moon' secreted away from greedy conquistadors.

According to history, massive amounts of gold and silver had been collected by the Incas from the four corners of their empire as ransom to buy the freedom of king Atahualpa, who had been captured and imprisoned by the Spanish conqueror Francisco Pizzaro. Atahualpa had struck the deal. Knowing the Spaniards' greed for gold, he stood on his tiptoes, reached his hand as high up the wall of his prison cell, and promised Pizzaro that in return for his freedom he would fill his cell with gold to the height of the line with treasure.

Blake had been inside that room. It measured seventeen by twenty-two feet, and the high mark was eight feet from the floor!

Yet, Pizzaro, insatiable for more riches, demanded that a second, larger room be filled. While loyal Inca troops were on their way with the convoy, Pizzaro reneged on his promise and, in a brutal act of betrayal, had Atahualpa executed instead. An Inca general got wind of this treachery and his troops took a detour, hiding the ransom, some said, in these very mountains. The hoard was a purported seventy thousand llama loads weighing some five thousand tons of gold and silver goblets of every shape and size filled with emeralds, rubies, and diamonds. There were gold replicas of birds, insects, life-sized mountain lions and llamas, gold and sliver rings, necklaces, sandals, royal headdresses, entire fields of golden corn adorned with sliver leaves and tassels, huge fountains of gold and silver encrusted with precious jewels.

Blake knew historical documentation held definite evidence of this second undelivered cache. And from what had been brought up from the bottom of the ocean from sunken Spanish galleons holding the first ransom, this still missing booty had an estimated value of five billion dollars! He fell back into the mud, wallowing in the enormity of the situation. This discovery, if proven true, belonged to generations of Quechua as a part of their heritage. For the world to see. Not for greedy tomb raiders or treasure hunters with get rich quick schemes that would either sell it or melt it all down for profit, erasing the history of the Inca civilization – forever.

If he notified the Peruvian police to guard against pilfering, even if they could be trusted around such vast wealth, they'd storm the site. A clumsy foot, even a carelessly handled or misplaced relic could destroy centuries old clues. He had to dig, covertly, get in, and photograph and record everything in its exact position.

Until then, Blake vowed to keep the knowledge of his find to himself.

Chapter Two

At the summit of the misty green mountain peak, Hope Burnsmyre rounded a knoll and suddenly faced tier upon tier of Incan agricultural terraces rising like a giant's green carpeted stairs to the sun. Each one, hundreds of feet long, was flanked by massive walls up to ten feet high. In her excitement, she forgot her fatigue and ran, stopping in front of huge stone blocks, seemingly glued together – but without the aid of mortar. She discovered it was part of a circular temple, and she took the small steps two at a time.

Hope emerged onto an open plaza of sparkly white granite set amidst an azure sky. As far as her eyes could see were row upon row of roofless Inca shelters that once housed twelve-thousand people. A whole, enormous city! All around the mysterious city jungle growth was alive with bird and insect song. She felt as tiny as ant on an elephant's back. Her rapid heartbeat stilled, awed by the spiritual majesty. Mountaintops Machu Picchu and cloud-capped *Huayna Picchu* cradled the ruins like the divine hand of the creator of all, known as *Virachocha* to the Incas. Thousands of feet below, the white rope of the *Urubamba* river thundered around a horseshoe bend on three sides. It simply stole her breath away – and in more ways than one. The experience was worth every blister, scrape, bug bite, and one nearly disastrous slip suffered during the brutal treks it took just to stand… here… in this magical, utterly astounding place.

A rangy man with a shock of snowy hair, a vested brown shirt, jodhpurs, and knee-high brown boots made his way to her. "Doctor Burnsmyre, I presume?" His warm brown eyes crinkled at the corners. "I'm Alexander Neville, an architect working under Doctor Sevenson. It's always such a pleasure to witness Machu Picchu again through another's eyes. Very humbling, isn't it?"

She blinked back tears of awe, and smiled, embarrassed. "Yes. It's such an honor to be here. But, please, call me Hope."

"Ah, yes… Machu Picchu." He took a deep breath and sighed in pleasure. "Built during the reign of the Inca ruler *Pachacute* in the middle of the 15th century, occupied, and for all the countless academic titles who've studied it and theorized, they still don't know why it was mysteriously abandoned after the start of the Spanish conquest in 1532." He extended a solicitous elbow. "Come. I'll show you to your quarters then… Hope." They traveled through a maze of stone halls, passing by the roofless shelters. "These housed the Virgins of the Sun, beautiful women who were a prominent part of the Incas religious ceremonies. Quite fitting. Your lovely presence does them justice."

He lied like a true gentleman. On a good day she would have described herself as pixie short, with her Irish father's green eyes, and even her earlobes and kneecaps freckled in the summer. After a grueling hike straight up in air thinner than angel hair pasta, her stomach growled at the thought of food. Her beige fatigues were torn and dirty and her thick hair resembled the red earth of Tara – after the war. As if an army of ants marched over her scalp, she could feel her hair frizzing out of her French braid. Why, she probably looked worse than the rain-soaked llama that had carried her gear, which had been more burden than beast. It spit, hissed, and plopped on the trail almost as much as Pedro had. And if she could choose between beasts – she preferred the llama.

Mister Neville led her into a roofless sanctuary carved into a vertiginous cliff. "I hope you don't find my compliment presumptuous? It's not often we see white women in our camp. Highland women are, well… poverty is a hard life that shows on any face."

"Oh, no. And, th-thank you," she stammered, more at her surroundings than from his praise. A canopy for rainy days shrouded one corner of the stone dwelling. Beneath it resided a rusty cot with a net begging for a bug-free tug into blessed sleep. Her gear rested on a granite altar rising from the center of a rock-based floor. The entry held a breathtaking view of the jagged mountaintops and – an aberration covered in mud from hair-end to boot-tip. Sunlight streamed around the muddy shoulders and a lion-like mane. The outline of the body was a black silhouette, but the height and stance were undeniably male. Hope squinted, trying to distinguish his facial features.

"Look what's risen out of the latrine!" Mr. Neville extended his arm like a circus showman. "Let me introduce my esteemed colleague, world-renowned archaeologist and explorer, Doctor Blake Sevenson. His initials suit him. And I'm not referring to bachelor of sciences. Although he is full of B.S. and a bachelor."

"I'm afraid Alex holds the highest degree of B.S. around here," Doctor Sevenson's husky voice set off an exciting tingle in her tummy. Hope realized she was somewhat awed that she was actually meeting

15

the famed, forty-two year old archeologist, although it was hard to tell if a grin or a scowl had cracked his mud mask.

Alex gave that crumbling cheek a pat and then shot her a wink before departing.

Restless energy seemed coiled within that large, muddy physique as he stepped out of the blinding sunlight and made his way to stop directly before her, which was definitely too close for comfort. Her nostrils were filled with strangely sensual scents; a potent combinations of sun, rain, earth, and hard work. Hope eyed a wetly shining, powerful chest of mud with manly dark hairs curling up though it. Feeling positively dwarfed, she tilted her head back to get a better look at his face. Dried mud there gave him the craggy aura of an unfinished clay sculpture. That same mud failed to tame wavy black strands of his shoulder-length hair. And, unlike Mr. Neville's polite and gentlemanly reference to not seeing a white woman for God knew how long, Doctor Sevenson's summer lightning eyes gave her entire body such a bold and appreciative assessment that her pulse reacted erratically and her nipples harden as if touched.

When his unusual eyes met hers again, she cursed her redheaded complexion. The hot blotches cropping up on her neck and face were always a dead giveaway. She took a wary step back to regain her composure, and he promptly thrust out his sloppy looking paw. She simply stared at it, and then gave a start when he snatched her hand from her side.

"Blake will do," he said in his rusty saw voice while wet grit grazed her palm in a firm, two handed shake. His tough-as-leather skin had calluses on the strong fingers that closed warmly around her palm and wrist. Unsettled by his hungry stare, overpowering presence, and her extreme reaction to him, Hope suddenly realized he was gently stroking her palm with the pad of his thumb, back and forth... back and forth... a slow, sensually hypnotic caress. She yanked her hand away, and swiped her shirt, leaving a mud stain across her palpitating heart.

As if nothing untoward had transpired, he turned to the stone altar where her bedroll seemed to loom. "It's amazing to think," his utterly masculine hand ran over rock formations that looked made to lie down on with depressions for the head, arms, and buttocks and... she imagined his fingers skimming her naked body in the same manner, "the last Inca king, Atahualpa, could have been laid out for burial on this very spot."

Hope suddenly wanted to die herself. A mindless hand massage from such an obviously healthy and virile male specimen who hadn't laid eyes on a red-blooded female for an eternity was understandable. It was also very flattering, but certainly no reason for her to act like those featherbrained female students struck by the silly hero worship he inspired throughout the archaeological community. "Actually..." Her voice squeaked oddly as she struggled not to focus on the tight buttocks showcased in impossibly dirty jeans. "I thought I'd be staying in one of the tents I saw from the plaza."

Sevenson snapped out of his strange preoccupation with the altar and turned to face her. "I'm afraid that would inconvenience my men. Most of them act like pigs and don't know the meaning of modesty."

"I see." Hope scanned the mud he wore so well. "Is there anywhere I could get a hot bath around here? After that hike, I feel as filthy as you look."

"The men wash in the mountain falls or streams. A warm bath is a luxury that takes up too much time. However, an Indian woman I hired by the name of Maypez will arrive shortly and show you to the temple bath."

"I'm sure she finds the term 'Indian' insulting," Hope asserted. "The people of the Andes have a right to their proper identity. They prefer to be called Andean or Quechua."

He raised a mud-caked brow. "Blame Christopher Columbus. Since few textbooks have corrected his mistake. Maypez will also see to your meals."

King Atahualpa's Curse! Was he was one of those professors who didn't care to be corrected? She was here, after all, to learn from him, but also here to contribute and assist him in useful ways. "I could probably eat a llama." She hoped humor would smooth any bumps on this trail.

"Llama meat is tough, but when sun dried and preserved in salt, which prevents dehydration on a hot dig, it can fill a gap and cure what ails you. And beef 'jerky' by the way, is a Quechua word."

"I'm sure anything else on the menu will be fine."

"Menu? Maybe you would rather stay in the *Ruinas Hotel?* It is the only lodging up here, but it offers all the comforts of home. Every modern amenity would be available to you."

"I'm not a pampered tourist on vacation. And I'm certainly not a grad student working up a resume, Doctor Sevenson. Granted, I may be here on my first field assignment," she made a rough point of unfurling and snapping out her sleeping bag, "but I'm here for the duration."

"Fine." He didn't sound convincing. "We're up at five a.m. sharp, Doctor Burnsmyre." He stressed her title as if it amused him. "But I suggest you make it six-thirty when you meet us at the dig. Maypez will show you where it is." He made his way to the scenic exit.

"I assure you, I'm quite accustomed to rising early like the rest of you."

"No doubt." He swung back around. "But unless you enjoy watching men in various stages of undress, you'll make it six-thirty. And wear two pairs of pants."

"In this heat?" she protested.

"We're cutting back on high jungle growth that's closing in on a dig near the ruins. The snakes are poisonous fer-de-lances that spring after their prey when disturbed."

Hope tried to puzzle him out through some sort of expression, but from this distance all she could make out were disturbing topaz eye slits peeking out of his mud mask. Was he purposely trying to intimidate her? Everything he said was to her benefit, but he made her feel foolish, which she guessed was his intent. "I'm not afraid of snakes or bugs. In fact, when I was a Girl Scout at camp, there was a locust invasion. I thought the whole thing so interesting, I mailed one home to my mother for her to save as a souvenir."

"Well, you'll find this campsite vastly different from the Girl Scouts. And we'll get along a lot better if you just follow my orders from now on, not question them." He turned on his boot heels, leaving two clumps of mud inside the portal to the clouds.

Why didn't he just add 'stay out of my way?' And why in God's name did she make that stupid Girl Scout remark? What was this anyway – an army camp? Who did he think he was! Did he treat everybody like this, or only her? No overnight rest in a hotel to recover from jet lag. An immediate ride on a decrepit train, squished into a ripped-up seat between farmers and her trail guide, Pedro, who smelled worse than the defecating dogs, pigs, and chickens also along for the ride. Top that off with a climb up a mountain in air so thin her every intake of breath involved inhaling that same malodorous guide who may have stolen some of her money. Oh, she had heard all the horror stories about unscrupulous guides, bandits, and even crooked police who framed tourists, but now that she was here, she didn't expect more insult to her injuries. And while she certainly didn't expect a red-carpeted reception, General Mud and Gall didn't even have the courtesy to meet with her personally upon arrival. He sent his architect friend!

Hope exhaled a disheartened breath. She had envisioned a patient mentor she'd romantically reminisce about in her far future, "And, I owe it all to the esteemed Doctor Sevenson' speech…"

Her stomach churned with the start of a migraine. She hadn't eaten since yesterday; too built-up to an all time high over knowing her final destination was at hand. She was exhausted to the bone, grungy, and now upset – thanks to Buzz Kill. Maybe everything would look brighter in the morning after a crash landing on her cot?

A heavy-set Andean woman entered her sanctuary. She wore a bright purple dress topped with an artfully woven, multicolored cape. Black braids dangled from a red rimmed, black stovepipe hat. Cheekbones dominated her weatherworn face. Slanted dark eyes scanned Hope as if she had personally brought the cholera epidemic to her country.

From her studies, Hope was fully aware of the highlanders' hostile attitude toward outsiders . Of course, 'The Great Gringo Sevenson' would be held in very high regard. He might personally find King Atahualpa's legendary treasures hidden in these hills from Spanish conquerors. These people believed such a discovery would mark the day the Inca nation would return to power and restore their dignity. She imagined Sevenson's head so blown up by their expectations and admiration over his lofty academic title – why, he probably took a bow when he heard thunder!

"I Maypez. You take *baño`*. You give money." Maypez extended her hand.

Hope dug into her duffel and produced a few sols. If Maypez wanted a little bonus above the wage Sevenson paid, she was going to learn English. "I am Hope," she annunciated.

Maypez accepted the tip with a gapped-toothed grin. "This way."

The temple was spacious and roofless. The stone walls may have survived the centuries, but the thatch above had rotted long ago. Yet what more could a weary traveler ask for? She would have a great view of the sky while she took a long, hot soak. She sprinted down stone steps to the steamy, four-by-four square bath level with the smooth granite floor. She couldn't shuck out of her grungy clothes fast enough.

"*Yuraq siki*," Maypez commented from behind her.

"Same to you," Hope replied. She knelt at the water's edge. Apparently, the Inca stood while they bathed, but the way her luck had been going, she wouldn't be surprised if it was a bottomless well.

Maypez set a small ceramic urn filled with a greenish substance beside her, and with a huff, she waddled up the steps and out of the temple.

Grateful beyond belief for the first moment of privacy she had had in days, Hope tested the water. She let out a yell that would wake the dead and yanked her scalded toes up from the surface. Oh, well, she thought. The sauna-like steam rising up to caress her face felt so marvelous on her trail-weary muscles, she didn't mind waiting for the water to cool. She sat back on her haunches and brought her long French braid over one shoulder. Mindlessly, she unraveled the thick, wavy coils. The action caused her hair ends to tickle her crotch like a lover's fluttery fingertips, making her aware she had lacked one for… why did it feel like forever? Even though her hairstyle was considered old-fashioned by scissor happy stylists, didn't most men prefer long hair? Yet with her cinnamon-brown mane wrestled into its ever-present braid most days, she had to admit not many men in her orbit saw the way the sun brought out the gold highlights.

In her last relationship, when she had let her hair down to make love to J.J. that first time, much to her disappointment he had turned off the lights. And he had pouted afterward; disappointed she was not a virgin like the other women he had bedded. Well, those other women weren't virgins now! She'd hung up on him, for two months; had never wanted to see or hear from him again. Why did she finally let him back into her heart and accept his apology? For a time, he had placed her on a pedestal, worshiped her, and was concerned for her well-being. First incident behind them, during courtship, he was quite the passionate lover, and they became engaged. But the closer their wedding date came, the more sexually distant he had become. At first she put it down to wedding jitters, but when all her attempts at seduction failed, Hope realized the terrible truth – J.J. had a Madonna-whore complex, or more apt a whore-Madonna complex. Love was for "good" women, and sex was for "bad" women. Sex before marriage was fine, but sex after marriage would defile his idea of the perfect wife. He would love, protect, and treasure her, but would not feel comfortable having sex with her once they married. It would be "dirty", like having sex with his own mother – the purest "good" woman in his life. And those twisted lines would blur further if children were ever born to such an unholy union. Thank God she had broken it off before she walked down *that* isle.

After that, it was no small wonder she had given up the practice of dating men with issues from within her academic circles. Most were sticks-in-the mud anyway, like Sevenson, threatened by her accomplishments or in competition. Mutual respect, trust, intimacy, romance and great sex seemed an impossible mix. The odds of ever meeting that "certain someone" she could really let down her hair with was about as likely to happen as the discovery of Atahualpa's lost treasures.

The ritual of letting down her hair to wash it usually involved an escape from her academic world with an indulgence in fantasy and self pleasure. Who needed a man? And here… in this utterly magical place… the whole Machu Picchu experience was enough to weave a sensual spell, even over the most jaded of scientists.

It was as though she could see through the steam curling up from the bath right into the past. The ruins were steeped in such mysticism, she felt like a Virgin of the Sun making ready for an Inca king. To think that that circular stone wall high above was once covered with the "sweat of the sun" that a life-sized mountain lion and llama forged from the tears of the moon once flanked the king's golden throne. Beautiful, dark-haired high-priestesses in short white tunics, gold sandals, and fantastically feathered head plumes hovered about in preparation for his entrance. Hope could almost hear the primitive beat of drums and the haunting sound of bamboo flutes… she could hear the soft, melodious voices singing songs of thanks to the sun god, Inti, made flesh incarnate in their Sapa Inca. Ceremonial plates bearing offerings of gold corn with sliver leaves and tassels were set inside those now empty niches carved into the walls. Gold chalices tipped into a jeweled, golden fountain spilled blessed water down those stone tiers and into this very bath. And she, the king's chosen, sat below it all, about to immerse her body and receive the restorative energies of those sacred, life-giving waters.

Digging Up Destiny

Hope scooped water from the bath and watched the droplets roll down her breasts. Her nipples swelled pleasantly as she welcomed the sensual images flooding her. She tweaked her rosy areoles into harder peaks and imagined high-priestesses attaching golden rings to each. A delicate loop of silver chain between them brushed her torso like a lover's whispered command. The king, she had been told, would hook a single finger beneath the chain, tug up and release, up and release, making her breasts bounce for his viewing pleasure. Breathing heavily now, Hope emulated the same lusty movements. Her tummy fluttered with excitement at the sound of his imaginary royal footsteps, coming ever closer in the ancient halls. As would a well-trained virgin of the sun, she knelt upright, arched her back, thrust out her breasts, and spread her thighs farther apart. How exciting to kneel submissively before a power that ruled over an empire more vast than that of the Romans! Would his eyes alight with pleasure as he took in the sight of her adorned breasts, her hungry pussy, all offered openly to him? And how long would he keep her on display in this erotic manner before he carried her off to his bed of soft *vicuña* blankets? She would not want to displease him and suffer his punishment. Although… thoughts of lying naked over his strong thighs, his fingers fiddling with her clit between smacks of his hand, spanking her hard until her flesh was hot and her body cried out for climax, could hardly be considered punishment.

Eyes closed, in her mind's eye she saw him enter the temple, resplendent in his gold crown and red robe lovingly fashioned by his artisans. Unbearable anticipation electrified her every nerve ending as attentive priestesses rushed to divest him of his silver travel staff, gold sandals, and robe. Before she had a chance to see his naked form in all its glory, the king quickly drew her to her feet in a rough embrace. His kiss was full of explosive passion as he rubbed his lusciously hard penis against her belly. Primitive drums beat faster and faster in rhythm with her heart and then the drums ceased abruptly and the king tumbled her to his bed.

Hope spread her labia apart with her fingers; a vestal slave opening herself to the Sapa Inca who would make her one with Pachamama, the earth mother. Her core craved the masculine energy of the sun. The feminine power of his consort, the moon, found that special sweet spot connected to the stars... right there... oh, yes. She pinched her clit imagining it was the gentle nip of the king's square white teeth. Under the intoxicating spell of his talented tongue, the little bud was lively, pulsing, hard, and demanding more. On the verge of culmination, his tongue vanished and he rose above her. Pressing two fingers steadily in the center of her labia, she slowly penetrated her slick, tight canal. His royal staff breached her imaginary barrier and was at last sheathed to the hilt.

Faster and faster, she emulated the thrusts of his fucking with her fingers. Deeper! She whipped her hair forward, a veil over her face, hair ends dangling into the water. Her fingers alternated, strumming her clitoris and then sinking deep. Riding the crest of a blissful wave, she thrashed her hair back in an arch of water droplets, hips reaching for his fantasy cock, reaching for release. The moment her muscles seized up, a loud screech sounded out and she opened her eyes to see a condor soar with its enormous wing span over the roofless temple. She took flight with "the messenger of the mountain spirits" and her own liberated cry escaped her lips. "Oh... Oh... Oh... Mm, yes, make me one with the universe!" Her head fell forward to her knees as if bowing to the Inca deities.

Reluctantly, she floated back down to earth and landed with a hard, unwanted reminder of J.J. He had accused her of having not only a too vivid imagination, but a too kinky one as well. And he had been right. Trouble was, she was so infernally in control of her life most days, she found the mere thought of submissively relinquishing that control to a dominant lover highly erotic. But to actually abandon herself to a sexually imaginative real man, without reprisal and guilt, to allow herself to be helpless, to feel nurtured, to release sexual inhibitions and a whole host of emotions was... wishful thinking. Her silly fantasies were not only outrageous, but thank Inti no one had been around to hear her cry out like some sex-starved nutcase!

Chapter Three

Hope quickly grasped the sidewalls and lowered her guilty body into the water. Her toes touched bottom and she stood in another sort of bone melting ecstasy up to her chin. The water was the perfect temperature now, just what the doctor ordered. She picked up the urn Maypez had left and took a hesitant whiff. The green substance smelled of eucalypti, and at a tiny dab of her testing fingers it lathered like mad. With a quick dunk under the water, she re-emerged, soaping her hair with the concoction.

"Maypez's insect repellant is generally used after your bath," Sevenson's amused voice drifted down from the ground-level stones high above.

Hope ducked with a splash. "What?" she burbled, lips level with the water.

"You're shampooing with bug-off."

She knew he couldn't see her naked body from the wellhead, but... "How long have you been there?" Surely he hadn't watched while she... her face flamed with mortification.

Sevenson's smile seemed obscenely large and ultra-bright amid his

Al Jolson-like mud-browned face. "I was just on my way to the falls when I noticed you... shampooing." He delivered a Boy Scout salute and vanished from her view.

Hope boosted out of the bath and jerked into her gray sweats and boots. She twisted her sopping hair into a pink towel turban, grabbed her dirty bundle, toiletries, and Maypez's bug-off. Like an Inca general on the march, she backtracked to her sanctuary, where she tossed her armload onto her cot, too ticked-off to ponder the odd addition of an oxygen tank.

Maypez entered her room and set a tray bearing a thermos and a large covered dish that contained a delicious smelling something onto the granite altar. "*Ope eat kkowi.* Drink *mate de coca. Soroche* bad."

"Take me to Sevenson," Hope demanded.

"Doc take *baño!*"

"Perfect."

Maypez showed no signs of cooperation as she unscrewed the cap to the thermos. "Doc says Ope need sleep."

"Did he now?" At first all she had wanted after her bath was a hot meal and about ten hours of drop-dead dreamland. "Take me to Doc," she insisted with a glower.

"Ope give money."

Hope slapped another sol into her palm, thinking whoever carved Maypez's character must have used a chisel.

Maypez led her through the Urban Sector. Hope must have counted at least fifty small and large stairways. She could chew every stone beneath her boots. The occasional cacti and thorny palm matched her mood. A tiny yellow lizard skittered from its sun basking into a mossy rock pile. The reptile reminded her of Sevenson.

The mere thought spoiled her delight at the still flowing Inca fountains everywhere she looked, yet hummingbirds hovering over red orchids and exotic blue blossoms in the Garden District were too beautiful to deny.

At the end of a long stone alleyway, Maypez pointed to a wooden outhouse.

Hope gratefully used it in a hurry. She emerged and muttered, "If it's your turn, Maypez, mention Doc's name. You'll get a good seat."

"Doc take *bano*." Maypez stabbed a gnarled finger at a downhill dirt path that tunneled into a ferny forest. "*Rupaq siki!* Gringo." She shot her the *mueca de Indio*, the Andean grin, and then left Hope to fend for herself.

Cultural studies had taught her the *Mueca de Indio* was a nasty grimace, not a genuine grin. It was a defense gesture against an alien world, the North Americans' equivalent of flipping someone off. Hope realized it was too soon to bond with Maypez, but she sighed at her failed objective regardless. She suspected Sevenson had done little, if anything, to pave her way with goodwill.

Neon green parakeets gossiped and preened from lofty perches of bamboo, cedar, and mahogany. Their chatter reminded her of Maypez ringed by Quechua maidens dizzing her at some religious festival. What did *sorroche* mean? Maypez had said it was bad. Could anything be good about today? *Yuraq siki* and *rupaq siki* probably didn't mean "Welcome to my homeland, friend."

Monarch butterflies took wing like a fluttering patch of autumn leaves. Hope grabbed a sapling before she slipped down a hill and those butterflies took up residence in her stomach.

Directly below in a miniature valley, muted sunrays streamed through the trees and danced diamonds over water falling from a grand rock fissure. The cascade roiled around mossy bottom boulders, emitting a high, fine mist of translucent rainbows that encircled a perfect pond. The only thing missing from this verdant paradise was the lion and lamb lying peacefully together. An imaginary snake flicked a forked tongue in Hope's ear, reminding her that the only woman without a past was Eve, because for all that was holy she couldn't tear her gaze away from the most exquisitely naked male physique she'd ever had the pleasure to behold.

Tree-filtered shafts of sunlight reflected off the water and shimmered over Sevenson's handsomely chiseled profile, his hard chest, broad shoulders, and sinewy arms. Without the mud, that masculine presence was even more virile, like Adam made golden under the sun. His dark hair, streaked with tiny silver wings at the ears, was plastered seal-slick to the middle of his sun bronzed back. The waterline simmered, boiling below his ivory sculpted buttocks. He sliced under the water and her gaze followed his shark-like path. How long, she wondered, could he hold his breath? Hope realized she was holding her own, lungs filled with a strange and exciting anticipation. When his head and torso shot up from the center of the pond, she nearly jumped out of her boots.

Sevenson shook his head and droplets flew from his hair in sparkly arcs. Calmly, he commenced scrubbing under his arms with a bar of soap.

Oh, God, even when he lathered up, his chest hair he gave all appearances of some erotic, primeval man of the jungle. She had the insane urge to place her hand over his, to follow the same slippery path in a worshipful way. He was so beautifully made.

Disappointment stabbed at her when he ducked back under to rinse. Soap bubbles ringed the surface, traveling to beneath the falls, traveling throughout her aroused body. What in Beelzebub's name was wrong with her? Hadn't she been about to climb down there to give him a piece of her mind? She'd been too fuming mad and wound-up by the Machu Picchu experience to think straight. She should make her presence known.

He emerged again, and that big hand trailed suds over his washboard belly and down further to swirl around his furry black thatch. She was positively possessed by some devil that made her gladly burn in all the best places. Her breasts ached to be touched and her swollen nipples longed to be licked. Her every nerve ending tingled like live wires dancing on a rain slick road. And that lonely wet road was located right between her legs. Her eyes flew wide when his hips gyrated in sensual circles. His semi-hard cock followed suit like some ritualistic primal dance he was performing, if she didn't know any better, exclusively for her. Impossible. With that water crashing down from the falls, he never could have heard her coming. His cock slapped one side of his pelvis, and then slapped the other side. His unabashed freedom of bodily expression was so male, so seductive. Hope knew it was wrong, but watching his magnificent penis grow while it swayed, almost whipping back and forth, made his excitement rise in her like the hottest fire of hell clouding her brain. The sight of his tight, soapy grip slowly moving up and then down his erection made her feel as if those masterful hands were massaging her vulva, radiating an intense heat there, a need to surrender, deep within her core.

What was she doing invading such an intimately private moment? This was so wrong! She forced herself to look away and to settle down.

Digging Up Destiny

He had only happened upon her in the temple bath when she had been shampooing her hair, she told herself, and not before, when she had masturbated herself. The man would probably be supremely angry if he realized she was watching him. If he caught her, he'd more than likely be mortified. And so would she, for that matter.

Hope turned to leave, but her mutinous eyes took one last look... and caught sight of the head of his cock bulging out from his tight grip like a ripe plum. He squeezed it, and the tiny red slit issued a tear as if his manhood was crying – no, begging – for her attention. A tantalizing shiver coursed through her and she imagined his reaction to a long lavish lick of her tongue. She visualized herself kneeling before him, satisfying his need with her hot flicking tongue, devouring just the luscious tip of him. She watched him cup his balls and bring the hefty sacs to the fore. Oh, what those remarkably deft fingers could do to the right woman! Was he saving up his sexual energy? Why didn't he just get on with it?

His masculine hand wrapped around his cock once again, moving up and down, faster and faster, the muscles in his handsome face tightening and relaxing, and those same bolts of bliss built inside her, the rhythm of sex beating in her heart. Oh, how she wanted that male hardness inside her, wanted that piston-driven, dominant strength possessing her body! The lusty vision of him working that rod had her squeezing her thighs together over her hand. His cock was so big! There was no way it would ever fit inside her. It was so...

Suddenly, he turned his head and looked directly at her. "You take your anthropology very seriously. Yes, I'd say you're very dedicated to the study of man."

"I-I-" she sputtered stupidly, and her hand flew away from her pussy.

"Don't take your hand away! Your show in the temple bath was so lovely. You looked like a goddess kneeling like that, so wonderfully submissive with your tits and your pussy all offered up openly to me... like a precious gift."

Her hands were on her hot cheeks as she struggled to shake out of her insane mesmerism. He was, after all, a complete stranger to her, not some mind reader able to tap into her outrageous fantasies...

"Come on in." His eyes twinkled with golden mischief. "The water feels great. And as you can see..." He shook his cock in an invitation of pleasure he undoubtedly could delver. "I'd loved to make you one with the universe."

His remark shocked her back to reality with an embarrassment so acute it made her see red. She was not a voyeur, she told herself, *he* was! Well, she would toss Tarzan a vine in the hope that he would hang himself. "Why, I'd love to," she purred like a feline in heat, and joyfully slid down the hill.

Knowing he watched her every move, Hope emphasized the sway of her hips down a short Incan stone footpath leading to the bank. With a dramatic sweep of her arms, she split the tall green reeds, and struck a hip-cock pose that would do a Vegas show girl proud.

"Ah, Hope," he murmured, stroking his impressive cock with an equally inviting gleam in his eye. "Lose that towel. I love the way your long hair caught fire in the sun. And those sweats, take them off, slowly, sweetheart. You're too beautiful for clothes. I want to enjoy every second of – whoa. What the hell are you doing?"

On tip toes, she had stretched for the branch where his dirty and clean clothes were flung, ripped them down, and bundled them up, taking great delight in watching his sexy expression crash. "I'll leave you your boots for the sake of snakes, but I hope the mosquitoes feast on your fanny on your naked journey home."

"Oh, come on, let's talk about–"

"And a fine fanny it is." She wiggled her brows and gave his granite buns a chauvinist once over. It was then that she noticed the high mist was in fact steam caused by cold mountain water falling into bubbling hot springs. "Looks as if your 'warm bath is a luxury that takes up too much-time' talk was a complete crock too, Doctor B.S."

"Don't do it." His glare was enough to freeze a hardened criminal in their tracks.

She tossed off a Girl Scout salute, spun around, and high-tailed it up the hill with his goods. She heard him cuss and crash through the water like an outraged grizzly.

"Get back here with those or I'll take you over my knee and spank that exquisite fanny of yours until you can't sit for a week!" His booming voice sent birds and frightened critters scurrying for cover.

When the path leveled to the ruins, Hope tried to catch her breath, but her lungs wouldn't respond; they were completely devoid of air. She dropped his bundle and clutched at her chest while cold, clammy fingers raced the length of her spine. Did some weird native insect bite her or, heaven forbid, one of those fer-de-lance snakes? Her stomach clenched into a nauseous knot. She swiped cold sweat from her face and glanced at her hand. She had never had a nosebleed in her life!

Searing pain stabbed her temples and her world tumbled into black.

Chapter Four

Hope dreamed she was hiking the Inca trail, struggling toward a pass between two summits. Out of breath, out of her element, she passed though a jungle. The entrance to a valley rose dramatically. She followed an ancient path spiraling along the mountainside and up towards the pass. A shadowy male figure dogged her footsteps, and yet in the way of dreams, he somehow taunted her to follow him. She stopped to catch her breath and to wait for him. She never saw his face. She followed and he pursued. Lost and unsure of which direction to take, like the mischievous Pan, he appeared up ahead. She rounded the knoll he had vanished behind, coming into The Gateway to the Sun. Machu Picchu was spread out far below. She had found the ruins by a trail she traveled with a companion she never saw. Suddenly her foot slipped on loose rocks and she plummeted off the cliff. Before she hit the ground, her soul left her body…

Her spirit hovered above her naked flesh lying on the granite altar in the sanctuary. Her face was a flat round mirror that reflected lightning fast images of other faces. Faces of relatives; faces of people she loved, people she disliked; boyfriends of the past; colleagues of present. The face of her future, like the faceless companion, eluded her. The mirror vanished and blue strings of energy shot skywards from her head, hands, feet, heart, stomach, and sex...

She was a condor soaring through blue webs of collective consciousness connected to the stars! Through bird's eyes she watched the blue webs twist into an umbilical cord. Following the cord's descent, out of the darkness of space, into the blue of the sky, she flew down, down, down to between the lush green mountains. Wings ripping through the wet canopy of leaves, she landed beside the cord attached to the rainforest's floor. The cord snapped free and took on the form of a writhing snake slithering into a muddy hole that resembled a freshly dug grave. With hooked beak, she tried to snatch it up, but the snake slipped beneath a granite wall. In the center of the wall, the golden face of the Inca sun god, Inti, warned, "Souls are as impenetrable to bodies as the barricade to The Cave of Tears..."

Quickly, she flew away, back towards ruins. Desperate to return to her body, she descended into the roofless sanctuary and to the altar. Landing on her chest – with a flutter of wings – she was back. Her eyes opened to sunrays beaming through the Temple of Three Windows. At the head of the altar stood an Inca king wearing a gold crown with red-plumes and gold discs in his earlobes. Small in stature, but powerfully proportioned, his broad, hairless chest, torso, proud erection and imperial ingots at the apex of his sturdy thighs were dusted in pulverized gold. He seemed a sun god sculpted from pure bullion, not flesh and blood at all, until he peered down at her. His flared nostrils and the bloodshot whites of his slanted dark eyes held the lust of ten bulls.

The king raised a stone sunburst aloft. Graphite particles captured the light and sparkled like diamonds. The lower half of the disc was missing. He set the half sunburst on her belly. His golden hand circled over it, faster and faster, until the gray stone became a golden swirl of intense heat that traveled deep within the tunnel of her sex. The stone vanished; his secrets hidden inside her. His lips did not move, but he spoke empathically. She understood but did not understand that she was his "chosen one" the keeper of a half made whole until he deemed the day of its revelation.

An emptied vessel; she would die for want and arousal or be filled by him. He smiled and roughly cupped her breasts, pinching her nipples to rubies, the jeweled transformation part pain, and part pleasure. His hands moved down, coming to rest over her vulva. Golden fingertips combed the crisp curls there, eliciting further bolts of exquisite heat through her veins. He unfurled her nether lips, and boldly watched her clitoris pulse like a sacrificial heart. Her cunt clenched with a clawing hunger. As if in answer to her need, he sank two golden fingers deep, pumped her slit, stoking her flames, increasing her fever to an unbearable pitch. Body trembling in a world of wondrous sensations, soaring over the edge of culmination, skin misted in a sheen of sexual heat, she cried out to him in his own tongue, *"Tukuy sonqoywanmi wayllunkuyk!"*

In the breathless aftermath of her orgasm, she meekly asked him to reveal the meaning, but the king touched one golden finger to her lips as if to silence her with his secrets.

Frustrated, she slapped his hand away from her mouth.

His laughter thundered throughout the cordillera. He sobered, tore away his headpiece, and tossed it with a clamorous clang that shot sparks across the granite floor. His hair resembled a condor's wings, straight black feathers that shone with the iridescence of an oil slick. He toyed with her hair hanging over the altar's edge. Then he gripped his gilded penis and pointed the bulbous head down to her lips. His gaze marched through her body, an army of thrilling sensations; she was powerless under his empathic commands. She touched his velvety testicles, gently rolling the nestled nuggets in her fingers, delighting in the different textures and the heady male aroma of him. She licked the salty liquid pearl at the slit of his golden cock, and then took the bulbous head into her malleable mouth. The king fed the proud shaft, inch by slow inch into the tunnel of her throat, the veins on his erection were like sun-warmed Inca roadways connecting the four empires throbbing with the heartbeat of millions.

With a guttural moan he pulled out, the gold gone from his cock, consumed by her greedy mouth, revealing all too human flesh. His vulnerable scepter swayed, shiny now with her saliva. She reached up for him, ashamed, desperately afraid he would vanish as well. Tender thumbs wiped away tears that coursed down her temples into her hair. Understanding and love enveloped her. Without words, he told her that the tears of Inti never had a monetary value. They were mere ornamentation meant to pay homage to the god who nourished precious crops, who gave life and warmth to his people. The creator of all, *Viracocha*, would never vanish, and like the beliefs of his children, the sun shone eternal.

His bulk dissolved into a shimmer above the hot, horny horizon of her body. Golden light descended upon her like the warmth of a languid summer day, then took on weight and form again, his penis a rock resting against her thigh. She gripped his granite buttocks and spread her thighs wide, welcoming the Sapa Inca home with all her being.

Silently, he filled her mind with prophetic words, opening his mouth over hers as her vulva opened to his erection. "You are my chosen, the keeper of the half." With each thrilling thrust of his penis, he planted confusing secrets inside her. "The Cave of Tears is not ready to be revealed. The past of my people is buried deep in the earth mother. You must ask permission of the apus to enter her womb. Pay homage in the Inca way. Pachamama surrenders her secrets when you are one with the universe. The past remains hidden until the one who digs discovers the true treasures of *waylluy*."

"Virile Sweet One!" she cried out his holy name as if she had always known him, as if he had been away on a long journey and had finally returned to her.

Moonbeams and sunrays shot from the conjunction of their fused bodies, renting the night sky in an explosion of gold and silver dust that rained down upon them.

"Help him to remember… remember… remember…" His seed echoed within her womb.

The heaviness atop her body lifted like clouds and mist burned off the ruins at the break of day.

Hope gasped for a breath and her eyes flew open. Blinking through the pain of a migraine headache, Sevenson's face came into focus. His worried golden eyes had curly black lashes women would kill for, and his beard-stubbed chin was marred by a thin red scar. Something was cupped firmly over her mouth. An oxygen mask?

Sevenson gave her a Boy Scout salute. "On my honor, I'll do my best to keep myself physically strong, mentally awake, and… I forget the rest. How many fingers are up?"

Hope shoved aside the mask. "Morally straight you're not!" she croaked.

His smile was replaced by a suspicious look. "I thought you didn't speak Quechua."

"I can't." That bizarre dream… she shook off her muddled recollection of it.

"Then why, when out cold, did you cry out 'I adore you with all my heart' in perfect Quechua?" he inquired reasonably.

"I can't imagine uttering those words to you in perfect English." She rubbed her throbbing temples.

"Glad you're back to your old self." He brushed away stands of her hair caught at the corner of her mouth. "But you're definitely not in Kansas anymore." His hand swept under her nape to raise her head off the pillow. Minus the mud, his damp locks shone, months overdue for a cut, yet the messy style only suited him. He placed a thermos cup to her lips. "Drink up. *Mate de coca* is a mild narcotic. An excellent remedy for *soroche*. Altitude sickness has been known to knock the healthiest of men on their asses."

"I'm not as spineless as spaghetti," she protested weakly.

"No. You're as temperamental as a twister."

She removed his hand abruptly and struggled to sit up, wincing from the effort. "Why do I feel worse than the morning after my brothers dared me to eat that tequila worm?"

"You've never heard of altitude sickness," he stated with a disbelieving stare. "Didn't the university committee brief you before you left?"

"I missed it when the airport bumped up my flight." She handed him the empty cup.

He set it aside. "Yes, but tourists talk about it all the time."

"I had my head in my textbooks for most of the flight."

"It figures," he mumbled.

"Pardon?"

"I meant it only figures you would be cramming about the Incas and their descendants."

Alex was right. The B.S. initials suited him. "And then I was too into the scenery on the train ride to bother with books. Besides, everyone gave Pedro a wide berth – if they had a nose on their face." She tested her own.

"*Soroche* sometimes makes an appearance with a nosebleed. Tilt your head back and pinch it so it won't start again." He gestured in kind, and then stood up.

The warm brew he had given her was beginning to do the trick. Her tummy was somewhat soothed, and the cobwebs in her brain began to clear. But with her head angled so, she became acutely conscious of his chest hair. It arrowed down his torso and disappeared into the pink towel she had turbaned around her head. Her face flamed when she recalled her voyeurism and thievery.

"It came in handy after I carried you here." He gave her a lopsided grin.

Mother of Moons, he had run naked through the ruins with her! Did Mister Neville or Maypez or any of the natives witness this? Why hadn't a poisonous snake bitten her? Maybe if she pinched her nose tighter she could suffocate herself.

"Your face is turning red again." Sevenson gripped her free wrist and pressed his fingers to it. "What are you...?"

"Shut up. I'm taking your pulse." The silent interval seemed an eternity before he released her wrist. "It went a little haywire when I told you to shut up."

"Your manners aren't half bad, they're *all* bad," she erupted.

"Another symptom of altitude sickness is a rapid heartbeat and rise in blood pressure. Highlanders are genetically adapted. They have larger hearts and lungs and about two quarts more blood. Some foreigners are unaffected. Others suffer from lack of oxygen when they first arrive."

She suffered the signs, but it had nothing to do with the altitude. He was too close. Too scantly clad. And minus the mud, too tall, dark, and hands all over her if she wasn't careful. "I didn't have time to experience symptoms. I had no overnight rest in a hotel, and before I could sneeze, I'd been shoved aboard and off the train to face this mountain."

"Which you tackled with all of your piss n' vinegar intact. An Olympian endeavor." Sevenson mulled this over in yet another puzzled assessment of her.

"My three older brothers haven't beaten my race times in the swimming pool yet."

"Lung capacity explains the delay in symptoms."

"How do you explain the fact that you didn't want me to make it this far?" she fired point blank.

He didn't as much as blink. "I had my reasons," he answered calmly.

At least he didn't deny it. "At this stage, I think I have the right to know those reasons."

"That's where you're wrong, Hope."

"How about you wanted me out of the picture, and out from under your big feet? Well, the Winslow Foundation is funding your expedition, and whether you like it or not," she angled a thumb at her chest, "I'm part of that bargain. It's also obvious you resent the inconvenience a woman will impose. That's called sexual discrimination. Need I go on, Doctor Sevenson?"

He stroked the stubble on his chin and contemplated her through hooded lids. "I dropped my professorship."

"It became retroactive the moment you cashed the first check."

"I suppose the Foundation folk think you're the best example of my learning tolerance."

"Insult me all you want. They would never have claimed you were once the best teacher. I don't know why you threw away, what is to me, a noble profession. It's none of my bus–"

"We're in agreement on something."

"Whatever the reason you became some mountain man recluse, I can't believe you would let it prejudice you before I've been given half a chance. I've more than earned my right to be here. Just as you once did, everyone must begin somewhere."

"Enough!" He held his hands up in surrender and his towel slipped from his hips. "I'm the wicked warlock of the western world." He caught it just in time, but not before resembling a sexy calendar shot for the month of May–heaven help her.

Her goggling gape shot to the overhead tarp. She'd never again pick a bone with this archaeologist. She wanted to lay her remains out on that stone altar until the sun fried her into a fossil.

"This gives the cliché 'caught me with my pants down' new meaning," she heard him say with a shameless chuckle. "Okay. I'm as decent as I'll ever be… under the circumstances."

She chanced a glance, and exhaled the breath she'd been holding.

"I think it's more than safe to say we've seen each other at our worst, and, ah, best." He scanned her quickly and beamed approval.

"Well, I think you look like a dork in that pink towel and those unlaced clodhoppers."

"I wouldn't be standing here like a dork if you hadn't stolen my clothes."

"And I wouldn't be in this predicament at all, if you wouldn't have spied on me like a pervert in the first place!"

He stared at his clodhoppers as if choosing his words carefully before he spoke. "Being on a remote mountaintop for three years can make a man behave as primitive as the natives. If it makes you feel any better, you were a sight for sore eyes, Hope." His riveting gaze, the use of her given name, and his honest admission, unnerved her with awkward mutual awareness. "I left the oxygen tank as a precaution. I assumed it was self-explanatory," he added, as if to fill the odd silence.

"Know what my mother says about the word *assume*?" she asked.

"Never assume, because when you assume, you make an ass out of you and me?"

"Fixtures of speech are only fun when you can speak them with authority."

A muscle quivered at his jaw. "How did mom take it when you mailed that locust home from Girl Scout camp?"

"Like a trouper."

"Her daughter must take after her then."

"Easy for you to say, now that you've seen me at my worst."

His brows lifted. "Do you think it's a good idea bringing that up? I wouldn't mind trying to convince you you're beautiful in your birthday suit."

Thank Inti he had the good grace not to remark about making her "one with the universe." They had a professional relationship with boundaries to establish and maintain... since they'd be working together... in very close proximity... for an entire year!

Maypez flitted into the room like an enormous butterfly during mating season. She took one hostile look at his half-dressed state and they began to babble back and forth in Quechua. Her gestures and tone scolded, and at times she was downright argumentative. Sevenson's explanations sounded contrite and conciliatory. "*Soroche* bad. *Ope eat kkowi.* Sleep." Maypez gently placed her rough paw on her forehead while she continued to bitch him out.

"Hi, Aunty M."

"*Warmichakoq*! Doc go!" She stormed out of the room in blazing Technicolor.

"Better not mess with my Mammy. What's *warmichakoq* mean?"

"It means I'm 'hunting for a woman'. I'm surprised she didn't pull my ear and make me go to my tent. I had a helluva time convincing her I wasn't about to seduce you."

Anthropology was defined as the science of dealing with humans, and she wasn't raised with two bachelor brothers for nothing. "Don't flatter yourself. You're not my type, Mud Head." How did he still manage a monopoly on virility in a pink towel?

"And what is your type, Ms. Hope of High Hopes?" he asked, amused.

She couldn't place him in a proper professor slot, didn't think of him as a brother, and he wasn't a patient, elderly mentor like Mister Neville. Oh, he had the fame she coveted along with the gray matter she admired. She had been told by many how she would learn more from simple association with Doctor Sevenson than from any textbook or droning classroom instructor. She had also heard about his uncanny ability to pick up languages with ease of a child. His autograph alone on her résumé could open a world of opportunities otherwise unavailable to her. He had the power to make or break her advancement with his letter of recommendation at the end of this field assignment. Of all the worse scenarios for an attraction. Was forbidden fruit destined to become her daily staple?

"Ms. Hope-of-High-Hopes?" Her mouth trembled with the need to laugh. "Why do I have this mental picture of a prissy, old maid bookworm living way beyond her seams?"

He laughed, a deep, infectious sound. "With Barbara Bush's pearls and Swartzscoff's boots?"

She pressed her fingertips to her tear ducts. "You'd never guess we're educated," she tried to say soberly.

"Mud Head is apropos," he said with a chuckle. "It's been a long day, for both of us, Hope." His tone was apologetic.

And his staying in her sanctuary any longer was inappropriate. "Right. Where'd Maypez go?"

"Off to the mess hall to re-heat your dinner."

"My stomach is not exactly up to it."

"Probably because it's empty. Roasted *kkowi* is a delicious delicacy. A treat served only on special occasions for families and honored guests. If you want to make it as an anthropologist, don't piss-off the natives. Just eat it." He turned to leave.

"I'm curious…" Was she out of her mind? Her question could wait until morning. She had a half naked man in her room that wouldn't mind trying to convince her she was beautiful in her birthday suit. And he had to be cold. The huge sun setting between the mountaintops had made the temperature drop dramatically. Higher clouds turned to fire with the other mountain peaks silhouetted on the horizon. A thin white mist hovered at the entrance of her ancient sanctuary like a ghostly specter. Goosebumps rose, not from the chilly air but from an almost supernatural sensitivity.

"I'm curious about you, too, Hope," his husky voice roused her from her daze.

She ignored the forbidden shiver of awareness. "Did I really cry out 'I adore you with all my heart' in Quechua?"

"You did."

A sudden premonition that somehow connected her intimately to Sevenson was too bizarre to voice. "I… I had this dream about an Inca king." He didn't have to know how sexual it had been. "It… it will probably sound crazy to you, but it left me with the oddest feeling of being suspended on the edge of time, as if it spanned the past with my approaching future… as if this king opened some mystical crack between two worlds." Had she unwittingly opened such a crack or was her dream a rational result of her bath fantasy?

"Freud has a lot to say about dreams," he remarked.

"He'd probably send me to a padded cell over this one. It was a real doozie."

"Most are. As far as the lingering effects, lack of oxygen can not only knock a person flat, it can make things seem fuzzy, as if you're drunk. In some cases, it can make one hallucinate."

"It's all so confusing, and I'm done in. I'm sure things will be clearer after a decent night's rest."

"You know," he said, thoughtfully rubbing his chin, "this dream of yours would be the perfect opportunity to make a connection with the natives. Especially given the fact that you spoke in the Inca tongue while asleep, yet claim to have no knowledge of Quechua."

"You're right! Andeans hold great store in their dreams and the interpretation of them."

"Yes. And there's an English speaking Andean shaman who lives in a nearby village. Roberto Diaz would make the perfect informant. I'm sure he'll help you figure it all out, as well as offer other meaningful insights into their culture for your study. I'll send a runner to arrange a meeting."

"That would be wonderful. Thank you, Blake," she said humbly.

"It's nice to hear you say my name without choking." His smile was even more irresistible now that their silly war was behind them.

"I guess you're not such a bad Mud Head after all."

"Once you get to know me better," he replied with blatant innuendo that told her a platonic friendship with him was a fully loaded gun in a game of Russian Roulette.

"I'm curious about something else," she admitted, "about something Maypez had said to me."

"Shoot."

"I believe it was *yuraq siki*."

"Maypez said you have a 'white rear end'."

Why did his answer have to involve her derrière? Her brain ignored the warning to send him off with a proper *adieu*. She simply had to know, although she'd amputate her tongue before she'd reveal the incident took place when she had gone down the hill to see him wash... among other delightfully delicious doings. "Maypez shot me the *mueca de Indio*, and said *rupaq siki*."

He regarded her carefully. "Trust me. You don't want to know."

"Oh, yes I do!"

"Didn't your mother ever teach you curiosity killed the cat?" He laughed.

"She also used to say 'satisfaction brought it back'." She jutted her chin.

"I think I'm in love with your mother. *Rupaq siki's* literal translation is '*hot rear end*'. But it's a phrase used to refer to a woman who is anxious to jump into bed with a man." His gaze clung to hers, analyzing her reaction.

Her blood pounded and her face grew hot. "Apparently Maypez has formed a gross misrepresentation of both our intentions."

"Apparently…" He sat on the edge of her cot, pulled her shoulders forward, and his mouth swooped down to capture hers.

Her surrender was shocking, immediate, and total, and once again her mind reeled with *deja vu*, as if this particular moment were predestined; as if she had always known him, and recognized the truth right here and now. The sun's red glow flooded the ancient sanctuary, and seeped into her heightened senses, as if she had a sixth sight; as if this enlightening kiss were a supernatural benediction.

His tongue tasted, tested, and then took with a mastery as challenging as it was rewarding. Dear God, it had to be the altitude making her this giddy, making this bond seem so right. Touching his hard, warm chest, feeling his rapid heartbeat and the soft hair curling through her fingers felt so familiar, having him so close that his warm breath fanned her lips… her common sense skittered into the eerie shadows.

He guided her shoulders back… back onto the cot. The reality of him took first place over kingly dreams as he stretched out beside her, whisked the towel away from his hips, and pressed his lusciously hard erection into her thigh. "You were such a vision in the temple bath, Hope!" In a heated rush, he nibbled on her earlobe, nuzzled her neck, and kissed the skin around the frayed collar of her sweatshirt. "I can't get it out of my mind. It's been driving me crazy!"

"I feel the same way about seeing you under those falls!" She returned his hungry kisses with equal vigor, unable to stop from falling under his spell.

"I want to be the one who'll bring you to your knees like that, so wild and willing."

And she wanted it, too, wanted to abandon her every inhibition to this oh, so real man, to become helpless, to lose control, to feel nurtured, just like in her outrageous fantasies.

He shoved her shirt above her breasts, clearly delighted at her bra-less state. Knowing he knew she wasn't wearing any panties beneath her sweats made her pussy clench with pre-orgasmic need. He stroked her nipples, circling with the raspy pads of his thumbs, the friction maddening her and making her mew. He squeezed her breasts together, and with a sigh of pleasure took the aching points into his mouth, first one and then the other, back and forth, back and forth, until she was ready to scream for mercy. "Christ. I can't get enough. I want to drive my cock between them. I want to fuck them!

"Oh, yes, I want to wear your cum!" Was that her voice, she wondered, as she gasped and mindlessly grasped his cock.

He groaned and moved her hand away. Clutching both her wrists, he raised them to the rusty bedstead and made her grip it. "Don't let go," he commanded.

Before she could blink, he pulled her sweatpants down and off. He tossed them over his shoulder, and then spread her thighs wide. When his head descended, she wanted to let go of the rail, wanted to touch his sleek skin, to explore the muscles of his back and buttocks, to taste and tease and suckle his nipples as he was tasting hers. His greedy mouth released her one breast with a puckered smack, and the rush of air cooled the saliva shiny peak. He maneuvered lower, kissing down her belly, licking her navel, making her whole body flush with heat. That emboldened masculine hand at her torso traveled to her pussy, palmed her mons in slow circles, plucked teasingly at her curls.

Without warning, he thrust a ruff index finger into her soaking sex, and smiled at her pleading mews. With a wicked gleam in his eye, he brought that finger to his nose and inhaled, savoring her scent, and then she watched him lick his digit clean.

Hope didn't think it was possible to be more exposed down there until he pinched her labia and peeled her lips apart, all the while staring spellbound at her sodden slit. He legs were forced wider still, and he buried his handsome face between them. His tongue flicked like a serpent's, licking and probing, exploring every slippery crevice. She thrashed her head from side to side, her hair a fiery halo on the pillow. His relentless tongue stabbed, lapped greedily, reveling in her salty taste, filling his nose with her potent scent, which only seemed to excite him more. She reached for his head, but he smacked her hands away, returning them to the rail, intent on her willing mental bondage; intent on tasting her surrender to the full. Her hips rose in the air and she began to buck faster and faster, keeping pace with his tongue. When a flash flood of submission drenched his lips and chin, he rose up and kissed her hard, making her taste herself.

"Open your eyes and look at me," he growled. His calloused thumb found the pulsating nubbin she had touched in the temple bath. Her eyelids fluttered against his unyielding gaze when he began to strum her clit relentlessly up and down and around. Breathing heavily, almost in a panic, she bucked her hips again. Her inner muscles seized up. "*Oh, Blake!*" she cried out his name as if he had somehow carved it into her soul.

Her body still trembling, he continued to torment her pussy, never letting up, and all the while she struggled to hold on to the cot rail, tumbling again and again over the edge of agonizing bliss.

"What is it you want from me, sweet Hope?" he spoke at last. "I want to hear you ask, no, I want to hear you beg me to fuck you."

Her dazed mind screamed for sanity. "S-top!" she gasped. "Th-this is wrong" Her hands flew down from the rail to clutch at his fast moving fingers.

He seized them and brought them to his lips, covering her knuckles with hot kisses. "You're afraid it's right," his husky voice alone was enough to unhinge her resolve. His hands slid into her hair, bunching it at the sides. His lion-like eyes devoured every feature on her face.

She squeezed her eyes tight against the site of him. "E-everything about you, and this place, this day, has happened too fast," she said, winded with orgasmic aftershocks. "This-this is not like me. I've never reacted this strongly to a man. Especially with a man I just met. It's wrong, I tell you."

"While nothing about you feels wrong to me, you're right. I'm not always the most well- mannered man." She felt his weight lift off the cot. "So, if you want to play safe, from now on I suggest you keep your curiosity about me in check." Her sweatpants landed unceremoniously on her chest.

Face on fire, she quickly sat up to slip into them. "You're the one who took advantage of me," she said, pulling her shirt down over her breasts with a jerk.

"You asked for it the moment I shook your hand, right in this very place. You didn't wipe your hand on your shirt because you were afraid of a little mud. You were afraid of your reaction to me. I think I know you well enough to say you're too honest to deny the nitty gritty."

She hugged her pillow and stole a wary sideways glance at him. The towel had returned to his slim hips, but the tented evidence of his arousal was still painfully apparent. "Finding each other attractive isn't necessarily an invitation to—"

"If it were as simple as that, Hope, we'd have been soaping each other up under those falls hours ago, and not coming clean with each other right now."

"I think I like you more the less I see of you."

"And you have a talent for telling a man to go to hell and making him look forward to the trip. But it's also a defense mechanism against your fears. Your witty remarks may send the all American college boy running for the safety zone, but they act like verbal foreplay on me."

"Who do you think you are? Freud reincarnated? You don't know me!"

"Maybe I recognize my own qualities in you. We're alike, in many respects."

"Respect has nothing to do with you spying on me while I took a bath. And opposites attract, Sigmund, not people who are alike."

"We have very different qualities when we're naked, don't we? And you're not a simple girl, are you?"

"I'm simpleminded for letting you seduce me."

"You're also a typical female filled with contradictions and mixed messages. And while it's been a delight discovering some of those mysteries…"

"I couldn't warm up to you if we were cremated together!"

"That's not what your body told me a minute ago. And explorers thrive on challenges – on the thrill of discovery. But by all means, keep it up, Hope, since I'd like nothing better than another reason to do more than kiss you and make you come in the palm of my hand."

"You!" She wished for a brick when she threw her pillow at his head, which he effortlessly dodged. "Don't you ever come near me again unless you want major complications in your life."

"You already are a major complication in my life, Ms. Hope-of-High-Hopes." He smiled. "And if it wasn't so late, and we both weren't so dammed tired," he spoke with an infuriating confidence, "I'd take you over my knee and spank that *siki* of yours like I should have hours ago."

Maypez hurried back into the room with a tray bearing a covered dish. "*Warmichakoq!*" she barked at Blake, and then added in a kinder voice, "Hope eat *kkowi*. Sleep."

"Enjoy your guinea pig, Hope."

"Guinea pig?" she squeaked.

"Guinea pig. Though it is neither from Guinea or a pig, it *is* a native rodent of the Andes." With a pat on her head, he turned and made his way to the rock portal, fading like a phantom into the night.

Maypez approached her with a sincere, gapped-toothed grin and lifted the lid.

Hope took one look and clamped the oxygen mask over her mouth.

Chapter Five

Every night while the world slept, Blake stealthy trekked, his flashlight guiding him to the "eyebrows of the jungle" where he had first discovered the wall bearing the gold image of the Inca sun god, Inti. Under the glow of strategically placed gas lamps, he had eventually uncovered the entire wall, only to find it impenetrable. Behind that damned wall resided gold and silver booty with an estimated value of billions of dollars. Historical documentation was all the proof he needed; the golden sunburst marked the hiding place of King Atahualpa's second ransom. The betrayed king's spirit seemed not only to guard, but to thoroughly bar the entrance to purported subterranean caves housing the last of the sweat of the sun and tears of the moon secreted away from greedy conquistadors.

Yet he had also discovered that a perfectly fitted rock in the shape of the sunburst covered the lower half of the golden image. The missing upper half of that stone plate had to be the way in. When the surrounding area resembled a blasted mine field of empty holes, he realized the only solution was to burrow beneath the wall and slide under like a snake.

Digging Up Destiny

As Blake dug, he thought about how treasure hunters still searched all over South American in vain for Atahualpa's hidden ransom. And the natives fed the foreigners gold fever, some claimed, to enact revenge on the Europeans who had conquered their ancestors' once great empire. A few who came close to finding it had either gone mad or had died horrible deaths. Many lost their way in the inhospitable mountain ranges and jungle swamps, victims, it was rumored, of Atahualpa's legendary curse. Blake wondered if he was cursed as well. At times he felt as if had he gone mad with that very same fever. Other times he wondered if he had become as obsessed with his find as his father had once been when working in the Valley of the Kings. He had only been a kid, but he would never forget how that project cost his parents their lives. He still had nightmares over the accident. He supposed it was only natural he had followed in their footsteps to become an archeologist himself. And despite battles with jungle rains, he had good reason to prefer the South American smell of newly turned soil over the dry dust and sands of Egypt where his parents lay buried.

Curses, gold fever, deadly obsessions be damned! Once his name went down in history as the discoverer of Atahualpa's lost ransom, at least their deaths would have some meaning.

Jungle birds set up a hell of a racket before sunrise, and at the sound of nature's alarm clock, it was imperative he get back to the camp before the men roused from their tents. Without a minute to spare, he made it to the waterfall in time to wash off the muddy evidence he wore. He napped there on the flat Inca stones of an ancient quarry until the sun dried his clothes. If he was lucky, he usually managed to catch an hour of sleep.

Hope was waiting for him as usual outside the ruins of Machu

Picchu at the Main Gate of the Western Urban Sector. As always, she was raring to go, impatient for their daily walk into a hole in the jungle wall. The virtual tunnel of greenery led to an excavation which was basically an Inca garbage dump, the location of the site he had been working on before he came across Inti's golden image. The Inca garbage dump had, however, produced, and still produced, valuable clues as to how the ancients lived on a daily basis.

Blake acknowledge Hope's wave, wishing again that she *had* been a horse-faced, Sherman tank and not this sexy imp with an amusing, barb-wired tongue, lively green eyes, and "here I come ready or not" female exuberance. Thoughts of her kneeling in a padding of hay with her shapely bottom up and wiggling, her freckled, dirt-smudged nose crinkled up in concentration while she used brush and tweezers to free history from a broken ceramic pot, still amazed him. She had really taken to field work these past weeks. If he got half the attention and excitement each minor find earned from her, it would only spell trouble.

Blake scrubbed at his face before coming up beside her. She was definitely his idea of every man's wet dream come true. Dressed in a straw hat, a white T-shirt that could have won her a contest in the overpowering humidity, army-green fatigues and brown shit-kickers, her compact figure could distract a ninety-year-old monk, and he couldn't afford these distractions.

"You're late again, Mud Head," she quipped, arms crossed.

"Thankfully Peruvians are the most patient people I will ever meet. In fact, they think nothing of waiting an hour or two for a friend. When will you learn that nothing happens here on time, *gringa*?"

"Jeeze. Someone woke up on the wrong side of the cot. A simple good morning would suffice. Or could it be you're afraid that eating your own words will give you an acute case of indigestion?"

"*Can* it, Hope. I had a rough night. End of story." And as they took the path in strained silence, he wanted nothing more than his cot and a three day siesta. He had been running on gallons of coffee and adrenalin, and keeping his find a secret from Hope and Alex added to that toll. He was usually open in all ways, but he simply couldn't take any chances with a discovery of this magnitude. Unfortunately, he had learned the hard way – loose lips could sink grants, life-long friendships, and tenures. The only right time to announce news of his find was after he broke into the caves and photographed and catalogued the contents. If he did so beforehand, it invited disastrous scenarios too numerous to ponder.

Alex wasn't much of a worry on that account; he was off on his own most days with his guide, surveying and studying the architectural wonders of the ruins. Hope was another matter entirely. Solely for her benefit, he had kept up appearances at the Inca garbage dump. But she couldn't be fooled as easily as Alex or his diggers. Eventually, she would become suspicious of his clandestine endeavors. And he knew full well she wondered what kept him from visiting her sanctuary at nights. The mere thought of her letting down her long, fiery hair, then finger-fucking her burning bush as she knelt before that steamy bath, drove him wild, and the memory of her crying out his name when he made her come, again and again, elicited a too obvious ache in him that needed assuaging.

Warmer, wetter, wilder than the higher altitude of the wide open ruins, the jungle ground was spongy, and at times they treaded on mats of leaves and interwoven vines inches from the ground. While she walked slightly ahead of him with that bouncy step of hers, his fingers itched to unwind her French braid trailing out of her straw hat over her backpack. The little rubber-banded fan of hair ends jounced enticingly above her equally bouncy butt. Her infernal braid switched back and forth like a tabby's tail as if inviting his hand to smack those sumptuous, smart-assed cheeks. And Hope had more cheek than the law allowed! If she knew how many times he had come close to turning her over his knee to deliver just the sort of warm-up she needed... He forced himself to look away before his palm made the rifle shot connection. The condition of his cock whenever she was this near almost made him forget the sheer magnitude and historical importance his secret discovery entailed.

Thankfully, Roberto Diaz would take her off his itchy hands. Roberto would escort her to the local village tomorrow morning, and not a moment too soon. The English-speaking Andean shaman would keep her happily distracted with anthropological insights for her cultural study. With Hope gone, he would finally have more free time in the day to break into the cave. It was a perfect solution that suited both their needs. Yet why did her imminent departure feel suddenly disconcerting, as if he was already missing everything about her before she even left? He had gone mad, all right. And even more insane, he couldn't help wondering about everything they could have been together. If only he hadn't come across that cursed sunburst.

As they hiked through the tunneled pathway, his men hacked away at the ever encroaching jungle with machetes, each stopping briefly to exchange cheerful greetings as he passed. These hardworking *campesinos* more than deserved the wages he paid them, which was ten times what they would earn from farming their land in these remote mountains. When he had first geared up for this expedition and hired them on, his additional reward system had been essential. Unearthing an object from their past gave a feeling of possession, and moral claim warranted compensation if it was to be willingly handed over in the name of science. It insured him against theft, and he paid them a divided sum an antiquity's dealer would pay for a stolen item. His reward system also encouraged good work, for if an object was broken during a careless excavation, no reward was forthcoming. The pick man usually spotted the items first, so he received most of the reward; the spade man half; the basket men who carried away dirt, a smaller portion. But that was then, and this was now, and his reward system would never apply when it came to the discovery of Atahualpa's lost ransom. With billions of dollars at stake, that knowledge could turn saints into sinners. Even in the remote Andes, a few rumors would draw scavengers and tomb raiders like condors on a llama carcass.

Hope broke him out of his musings. "Hearing them sing songs to Pachamama while they work always warms my heart. If only I could understand all the words."

"They're singing about how the earth is their mother that gives them food. The lyrics go something like this... from Mother Earth come water and life. Our past comes from her. We live the present on her and our future will always depend on her. Pachamama is used by man and beast and plants grow on her. She must be cared for and loved, for without her, humankind could not exist."

"That's as beautiful as their belief in *ayni*," she warmed to the subject, "which I know means, 'Today for you, tomorrow for me'. *Ayni* was practiced in Inca times, and if my textbooks are correct, it means being able to live with Mother Earth, sharing her land with the animals, sharing all things as if brother and sister in the spirit of reciprocity."

Blake grabbed her arm and held a prickly branch aside so she could pass through without a scratch. The pulse in her little muscled bicep raced beneath his fingertips. Her jungle-green eyes searched his, and all the blood in his body headed permanently south. He wanted to kiss every freckle on her flushed face, taste the tiny bead of sweat pooled in her collarbone, tumble her to the ground and sink his cock deep into her cunt. "There is no separate self with them," his said hoarsely. "Quechua even speak in the third person 'we' instead of the first person 'I'."

Hope broke his horny hold on her arm to precede him on the path. "There's something to be said for sharing all the work so that each man benefits from helping the other."

He recovered the few cells left in his lust-fogged brain. "Their belief in *ayni* makes for good neighbors. I help them in whatever way I can, and in turn they helped me to build my humble abode in the Sacred Valley of Rainbows. I'll never tire of their stories, the singing and dancing during festivals honoring nature. More than a few times they plied me beyond inebriation with their homemade beer." He chuckled. "*Chicca* is made from their yields of *sara*, fermented from corn. You'll have to try it sometime."

"Why, Doc," she used the natives' term for him, comically batting her lashes over her shoulder, "is that an invitation to a cocktail party at your place?"

"I'm sure you'll get more than your fill of *chicca* when Roberto Diaz gives you a tour of the ruins tomorrow," he replied, and then hated himself for the sudden death of her flirtatious smile. "According to Maypez," he amended, "this master shaman's a forty-year-old bachelor who makes Quechua maids and maidens swoon with love for him under his magnetic spells." He actually felt an uncharacteristic stab of jealousy that twisted in his gut. "Maypez boasted that he scaled the highest, most sacred of the Apus, a snow-capped mountain where natives make their annual pilgrimages. She said Diaz had been struck by lightening, and descended the icy mountain unharmed, giving witness to his miraculous vision quest."

"What interests me more was what Alex had to say about him. Roberta Diaz is Q'ero. The Q'ero people were the very last of the Incas – a small group of six-hundred who escaped the Spanish conquest by seeking refuge in the highest mountains. Can you believe the Q'ero only came to the attention of anthropologists in 1949 after centuries of hidden isolation? For over five-hundred years, Q'ero elders have held a prophecy predicting a time of great transformation, *pachacuti*, in which harmony will be restored to Pachamama and her human children."

"*Pachacuti* translated means 'earth' or 'time'," he offered. "*Pacha* 'to set things right', *cuti*, 'time to set things right'." He wondered if he should do the same with her.

"Alex said Roberta Diaz is a fifth level *pago*, or shaman."

"Medicine man, priest, healer, and witch doctor, it's all the same to me."

"Of the highest variety taught by master elders from birth! How can you downplay it? *Pago's* hold great store in the myths, stories and prophecies I'm familiar with. They work with ancient traditions that predate modern medicine. Roberto lives adventures that defy common sense and the norm! I think these shamans give outsiders permission to free the subconscious child within us that our western education stifled and our culture has all but forgotten."

"So, this shaman will take you into a new and beautiful world you've only read, studied, or dreamed about, is that it? He'll dazzle you with ritualistic practices using rattles, feathers, fetishes, smoke and-"

"They *camay*, or 'breathe unity into', blowing smoke over the body, or whatever it is that's out of synch while they call on natures' deities to put it back in order. It's kind of like nursing a sick houseplant back to health. They use earth's energies like crystals, herbs and plants to connect mankind back with nature and Mother Earth." Like the umbilical cord in her dream...

"I know *ayni* is not some hocus pocus New Age religion to them, it's a philosophy of life, a symbolic way to live spiritually connected to the earth, the moon, and—"

"And all the worlds in between!"

"Last I looked I was standing on one." He indicated the ground.

"*Pago's* see visions of parallel worlds and spirits through *gamay*, 'the third eye'."

"I can see fine with the two I have." And when it came to Hope, he liked what he saw, trouble was she seemed a little too receptive.

"Shamans use ancient energy medicine practices to help release blocked or heavy negative energies like you have right now," she went on. "They can eliminate past mental trauma trapped in their client's aura and restore balance to the seven main chakras in the body." Like the blue strings connected to her body in her dream...

"So you think I have too many negative energy fields?" He glanced down at hismself.

"Well, something's stuck in your craw field that could stand to be removed."

"Look, Hope, to Andeans, in general, the condition of their world depends upon the condition of consciousness and of soul and a complete balance with every living thing. They believe the universe reciprocates every action of a person, good or bad, like a mirror that reflects intent back to act as mirrors to others."

Like the collective consciousness mirroring the many faces in her dream? Roberta Diaz would not only interpret it, but he would surely clear up the lingering confusions. He most certainly would not think of her, or her dream, as crazy. "Shamans live, walk and breathe the otherworldly. Of course, you'd think its all hogwash, scientific minded stick-in-the mud that you are. As for me, I can hardly wait to meet him."

"Now, now, sweet Hope-of-High-Hopes, I don't mean to put a damper on your open-mined anthropological brain and enthusiastic heart, I'm only saying a healthy amount of skepticism's in order. I've journeyed with master shamans both in the mountains and in the jungle. They live in synchronicity with nature, true, but some use mind altering plant extracts to psycho navigate in so-called parallel or supernatural worlds, one of which is a dangerous brew called 'The Vine of Life' or death, depending on your view. So, whatever you do, *don't* drink the water."

"Have you tried this brew?" She cocked a brow.

"It makes you throw up and then hallucinate for twenty hours. Stay clear of it."

"I've heard of this practice," she said, intrigued.

"I don't like that look in your eye. Maybe I should send Maypez along with you."

"Mammy's too old and portly to be traipsing around after me."

"Why do I have this itch to smack that cute little *siki* of yours?"

"I'm surprised the shamans you met didn't teach you to purge such negative thoughts and actions." She gave him a look that could be poured on waffles.

"When it comes to you, I would hardly call the action I have in mind negative." He laughed, and then sobered. "The *pago's* I met were truly devoted men, Hope, and true shamans have a great deal to teach us. They show others how to reflect goodness and receive the same balance back in what they refer to as the 'Circle of Love and Light'."

"So what are you worried about?"

"The flipside uses black magic to prey on the vulnerable. Witch doctors, or *bruja's*, slip men Mickey's and steal wallets. A bruja will seduce a woman while she's under the influence of their potions." And steal an innocent, too trusting girl's heart, he mused.

She snapped off a cluster of purple berries she passed, twirling it as if it contained some missing link, and then casting it away. Much like his mindset when it came to her, green and yellow parrots argued in the canopy of crisscrossed vines and tangled Spanish beards that hung from dripping mammoth leaves. Sunlight shone through in places like stage lights, giving Hope the appearance of a feisty Irish wood nymph with her bouncy red braid and green fatigues. Hummingbirds fed on dewy red orchids as beautiful and succulent as her sex. He wanted to take her off the beaten path to a needle thin, icy waterfall that fell hundreds of feet from a mossy rock ravine into a sparking lagoon. A white butterfly alighted on her kissable shoulder, and she stopped in motionless enchantment for a second until it fluttered away.

"To know the artist is to study his art," she breathed as she took it all in. "No human hand could have designed such a sophisticated system, or such a variety of beauty. I can understand why you left North America behind to embrace this."

"Last time I stepped foot on home soil, the skyscrapers, the traffic, the parking lots filled with cars, the fouled air, the polluted rivers, and the decimated forests... they all closed in on me."

"Like a bad case of culture shock in reverse?" She smiled over her shoulder.

"I wondered where all the smiling faces were in the frantic race for a better life."

"Most get the saying wrong." She tore off an elephant ear leaf and tickled his nose. "Money is not the root of all evil, it's the *love* of money that is."

"Well, these folk consider themselves far from poor in paradise." He swatted the leaf down. "I'll never forget what a wise old grandpa once told me. He said, 'A person's value is not measured by the amount of corn in his fields, but by the sunshine in his heart'."

Hope's reply was cut short when they stepped out into the treeless, sunny clearing. Blake was hard pressed to spot the top of the ladder poking out of the deep excavation from the ground growth yet to be cut. When he pointed this out to a few *campesinos* taking an overlong siesta, they teased him again over his naked dash through the ruins with Hope. He had been unable to wait; they called out in Quechua for him to carry his new girlfriend off to bed to fuck her. Two of them pulled at their hair and then pointed to Hope's.

She elbowed him for an explanation. "What gives?"

"Most Andeans have straight black hair like their Inca ancestors, so they like to poke fun of anyone who happens to have curls."

She waggled her humidity frizzed braid at them, setting off more hoots of male laughter and rowdy comments.

"They're saying it's the color of pumpkins."

"It is not!" she protested self-consciously. "Only my hairstylist knows... its cinnamon brown with golden highlights"

"Too late. You've just earned the honorable nickname of Pumpkin Head."

"If I'm a Pumpkin Head," she grumbled, "tell them you are most definitely a Mud Head of the highest caliber."

"Don't take offense, sweet Hope-of-High-Hopes." He gave her braid a yank. "Didn't they teach you anything at Stanford? Playful insults are forms of recreation with *campesinos*. In fact, competitions often arise between insulters, each trying to make the other appear more ridiculous. And," he sang, "considering your sharp tongue," he handed her a machete with a dirty grin, "you should feel right at home."

She shot him a glance that could wilt jungle growth, and then gave the waist-high bush between them a wild whack with her weapon. He wisely jumped back before she mowed him in half as well, laughing at her antics along with his diggers.

They shared an easy camaraderie, Hope thought, when they weren't busy lusting after one another in frustrated silence. Altitude sickness behind her, she wondered how she had managed to drag herself out of her sleeping bag that first day. Dressed against fer-de-lance snakes in a long-sleeved shirt and two pairs of pants, she would have lost her weight in water in this heat without ingesting salt tablets. And the straw hat Blake had also gifted her with kept her brain from cooking beneath the merciless sun.

South America had changed her. She had been taught to keep warm with heaters, stay cool with air conditioners, run for cover when caught out in a storm, hide from lightning, seek shelter from the wind, and to never play in the mud or get dirty. Ice capped mountains like frozen moonscapes were mere hours away from lush, tropical jungles. Hiking down from the ruins on ancient Inca trails, there were some chilly mornings when they had to shed layers of clothes along the way. She quickly came to respect and appreciate the elements of nature and vast weather changes.

Right now she prayed for the intermittent jungle rains that would cool her off while working... if only that rain would work as well on the heat Blake evoked between her thighs. Their sexual impasse had created an unbearable tension that grew thicker and faster than the jungle. Every accidental brushing up against the other, his hold on her arm before she scratched herself silly on a thorn bush... all of it reacted like hummingbird wings on her clit. At least today she had the luxury of standing yards apart so they wouldn't accidentally slice each other into ribbons with their machetes. Still... how many sleepless nights had she spent thinking of him, by turns exasperated with him and longing for him. She had to face facts – she had fallen hopelessly in love with him.

Her thoughts filtered back to a day in his laboratory tent. He had dabbed her scratches with a cotton ball of peroxide. His calloused fingers looked strong but were so gentle, and in the unsettling closeness, she found herself needing oxygen again because she had forgotten how to breathe. His hazel eyes caught and held hers, hot and expectant. His chiseled lips inched closer, his gaze fixed on her mouth. Her pulse tripped, she nervously licked her lips, and then his mouth was there, covering hers, warm and firm. He licked her lips, teasing them open with a tantalizing tongue. Then he entered her mouth slowly, just over the edge of her teeth. She opened her mouth farther, wanting his tongue, wanting all of him. He was spilling peroxide on his boot when suddenly a Quechua boy rushed into the tent, breaking the spell between them.

"Doc!" he sobbed, clutching at his bloodied knee, and Blake caught him up in his arms, lifting him onto the table. His soothing, deep voice stilled the boy's tears while he washed and treated his wound.

Her heart squeezed in her chest when she watched him wind sterile muslin, normally used to wrap fragile artifacts, around the boy's knee.

"I keep telling the *campesinos* I'm not a physician, but a doctor of sciences," he explained, "but they don't understand. To them the title 'doctor' means 'healer'."

So that's why they called him Doc. How wrong she had been about his having given himself overblown academic airs. "Does this kind of thing ever interfere with your work?"

"Sometimes, but how can I refuse? They're too poor for real medical care." He smiled at the boy's look of expectation, and fishing in a drawer, he produced a rare candy bar that set the child's face aglow. "When I first came, I gave him my ballpoint pen. He'd never seen one. I had to show him how it worked. One thing led to another. He's writing his name in Spanish now. These kids are like sponges, so thirsty for knowledge."

So... he had compassion. He really cared. And he had found students more in need of his services. Hope knew then that Blake Sevenson was much more than just another illegally handsome Mud Head.

The boy yammered with a mouthful of chocolate. The foreign conversation was a mystery to her, but the mutual affection between man and boy was quite clear.

"Kosi's name means 'happy'," Blake told her, laughing at the boy's exuberance. "He says he knows the meaning of the white lady's name and that it's a good name. He's saying his people 'hope' their legends will come true. He says, 'We hope you will help Doc find the treasures of the Incas buried beneath the earth mother', and he asks, 'Are you the chosen one who will return the gold and silver to the Temple of the Sun so the Great Inca Empire will rule again and his people will be victorious'?"

"Tell him I'm just a humble servant of Viracocha, not his chosen, but if I find the treasures, I will also help Doc return them to the *Cuzco Museum* so all the Children of the Sun may see the greatness that once ruled here."

Blake translated, lifted him down, and swatted Kosi happily off on his way. He then picked up a knotted colored cord from the table, and tossed it over to her. "As you know, the Incas had no written language."

Hope fingered the cord, recalling the umbilical cord in her dream of the king. "It's a *quipu*." She looked up at him. "They aided memories trained to preserve tribal history, songs, and the rituals present day Andeans keep traditionally pure."

"The Spanish conqueror, Pizzaro, burned the *quipa* libraries, which would have told us a lot more about the Inca than we know."

"The secret of reading the records died in the conquistadors' fire," She agreed grimly.

He nodded. "Other than a few written accounts by the Spanish, all we have to go on is their legends. So your knowledge of their legends and stories might be a valuable aid that will hopefully fit together more missing pieces of the puzzle."

"Digging up destiny... isn't that what archaeologists and anthropologists do best together?" she asked, and missing pieces of her dream rushed into her mind. Lost and unsure of which direction to take, she had found Machu Picchu by a trail traveling in a cat and mouse game with a faceless male companion. And the mirror that flashed faces from her past and present had vanished before it revealed the face of her future. In that fully conscious moment in Blake's lab tent, she looked lovingly upon his unaware face, all the while longing for his kiss.

Hope's eyes welled at the memory, but she refused to shed a tear over that sexy oaf! She swiped at her face and grasped a vine growing into the excavation. The whole thing resisted, and made her think that a clinging vine was something she would never become. She chopped away at it as if to kill the horrid thought. She needed to focus on her career, and Blake made her lose sight of her main objective. Meeting Roberto Diaz tomorrow was an absolute *raison de' taint* for an anthropologist.

Like some dark omen, a fer-de-lance snake suddenly sprang up out of the brush. With a scream that would curdle milk, she dropped her machete and half ran, half stumbled, backwards straight into Blake. Knocked off balance, he fell back and dropped down ten feet with her into the Inca garbage dump, where they both landed with winded huffs on a bale of hay used to pack artifacts into crates.

Hope stared in stunned silence at high dirt walls festooned with roots and moss. Quechua diggers appeared at the top of the deep hole. Dark, slanted eyes set in classic Inca faces peered down at her where she rested astride Blake, both of them sprawled flat in an explosion of hay. One native imitated her scream, and jumped up into another's arms. Accompanied by the sound of their laughter, she climbed off Blake with as much dignity as she could muster.

Hours later, Quechua men hoisted the umpteenth basket of dirt up by ropes and out of the excavation. One man shoveled more dirt into her boxed sieve, mounted on swing chains between sawhorses. He made his way up the ladder to disappear over the side, and Hope squinted at the white hot sun. She wished for a single rain cloud in the brown circle of clear blue sky. In fact, she would donate her overactive hormones and Blake's gonads to science for a hearty downpour that would cool off her clammy body. She envied Blake's shirtless state where he knelt one level below her. He reminded her of a happy kid with a trowel digging around in his favorite sandbox. He certainly didn't look any the worse for wear in the miserable humidity. Unlike her frizzy, sweat-soaked hair, his dark ponytail was dry as a snake weaving its way between the even dryer desert of his sun-bronzed shoulders.

She continued to rock her sieve like a bored miner panning for fools' gold. Back and forth, back and forth she rocked it with the monotony of a metronome. Sifted dirt grew in another pile beneath the box, leaving more empty yields of bothersome rocks, not anticipated artifacts, in her screen. Round and round she swung it and her eyelids grew heavy. She needed to think about something, anything, more entertaining to keep awake.

Round and round she swung the sieve, reminding her of the way Blake had relentlessly brought her to repeated orgasms with those deft fingers that, unlike her, freed history, not rocks, from the earth. Back and forth, back and forth his naked body would have moved over hers, his formidable cock thrusting inside her wet pussy. If only she wouldn't have slammed on the brakes that first night in her sanctuary! Was he tormenting her on purpose because he thought she was a tease? Well, she wasn't one of those loathsome creatures who, after experiencing her sexual pleasure, cried virtue, leaving the poor guy frustrated and unsatisfied.

She plucked out rocks from her screen and tossed them away. She frowned at a big ball of clayish dirt that refused to bust loose. She stabbed into the clay with an awl, and after the fourth careful probe, she commenced rocking the sieve, all the while stealing glances at Blake's oh-so-fine fanny peeking out from his jeans. Corded muscles rippled across his shoulder blades when he drew back a blue chalked string, and snapped it to the ground, marking off another key section of unearthed artifacts. One more snap, and the crisscrosses of blue lines brought to mind the blue webs of collective consciousness in her dream. Mesmerized by them, she almost missed it when the ball of clay broke into pieces and scattered across the screen, revealing half a stone sunburst which, when whole, would be around the size of a dinner plate.

Her elbows locked and her knuckles whitened at the edge of the box. She could scarcely believe her eyes as Inti's carved eyes stared back at her. As if surgically sliced in two, the sun god's mouth, chin, and lower rays were gone. Her vision began to blur and her heart was beating too fast. A locust-like hum in her head became increasingly loud. She closed her eyes to steady the dizzy spin of the disc, and in her mind's eye she saw the king dusted in pulverized gold standing in the sanctuary just as he had in her dream.

"*Mamacona.*" He greeted her with an imperious nod. "Keeper of the Half."

She felt his hand circling over the very same sunburst on her belly until the gray stone became a golden swirl, fluttering like thousands of butterflies and arousing her as if someone had slipped her an aphrodisiac. And then the disc vanished as if he wanted his secrets hidden inside her...

Then, she saw Inti's gold image in the middle of a stone wall shrouded by mist. "Souls are in danger of becoming impenetrable to their bodies as the wall barricading the Cave of Tears…" The words ripped into her subconscious. Assaulted by brain waves not her own, the fact that she was re-experiencing her kingly dream while awake almost short-circuited her reason. "Leave me be!" her mind screamed, and the amplified hum in her head stopped abruptly.

Hope opened her eyes. Her eyesight was fine. Her hearing was fine. She was fine. But she was thinking too fast and not thinking at all. The king called her '*mamacona*', a "chosen woman" a "virgin of the sun" trained in ancient arts dedicated to serving the sun god made alive in him. She had imagined herself as one in the temple bath when she fantasized about an Inca man making love to her; making her one with the universe. Some of made it sense and none of it made sense. The Cave of Tears sounded like an Inca place of worship, but it could be one of thousands located in the Andes. Either her brain had bounced and swollen when she fell and landed on Blake or she was going off her rocker. Heat exhaustion? No. She had already drunk three canteens of water. The altitude? That had to be it. Her oxygen-deprived brain went off on some weird hallucination. No… she was a sane person; an anthropologist with a well-trained rational mind. The dream state she had just consciously experienced had been an encounter with a real force that left her with a premonition of danger too real and powerful to ignore.

She scanned the excavation for diggers and came up empty. Before Blake could see what she was about, she plucked up the stone sunburst, knelt on the ground, and slipped it inside her backpack.

On her feet in a flash she gave the sieve a few more nervous shakes, making sure there weren't other finds in it that might fill her with such a terrible foreboding. She was a *mamacona*, the keeper of the half made whole until the king deemed the day of its revelation. Even if she didn't understand the whys of it all, she felt honored and empowered, and also incredibly burdened by the responsibility.

"What do you think?" she asked Blake in the most causal voice she could feign. "Did the conquistadors make off with all the Inca gold, or do you believe the legends that say much of it's hidden in these mountains?"

He brushed chalk off his hands, stepped up to her level, and made his way to the other side of the sieve. He plucked his canteen off a rock shelf, popped the top with a thumb, and guzzled. Water sluiced down the sides of his chin while his Adam's apple bobbed. He doused his nape with the last of it, and sparkly droplets ran down his chest. Lusty memories of his naked body under the waterfall bombarded her senses.

He glanced down at her empty screen, and pinned her with a golden glare, dark smudges beneath indicating he'd had a rough night. "I suggest you quit day dreaming about buried treasure. It sounds as if you're too wrapped up in the romantic aspect of archaeology to be objective scientifically. What we uncover here is an intellectual inheritance. The opening up of the world affects us all. The past is our legacy."

"I was just making conversation!" She put her hands on her hips, just as hot and bothered, and tired. "Can I help it if I was bored digging up rocks and sifting through dirt as if it contains the missing link? Don't tell me you wouldn't enjoy finding Inca gold, too."

"The value of a relic isn't whether it's gold or silver, but its history. And history is priceless." He stabbed a finger down at a chalked blue section of uncovered shards. "The gold you dream of finding is worthless next to that cracked ceramic face that shows us exactly what the Inca looked like."

The circle of sky above suddenly darkened, casting them in shadow inside the dig. Seconds later, heat lightning illuminated their stormy expressions.

"I'm well aware of that, Mud Head." She lifted her chin and their eyes locked to the rumble of thunder. "It's obvious there's nothing here at this level," she scoffed. "We should be digging down further instead of wasting our time here."

"We have to be absolutely sure this particular level contains no relevant history before we dig down further!" The dig darkened and lightening flashed again. "Once the men carry away this dirt, *that's* it." He snapped his fingers. "It's history; gone forever."

"Who do you think you are, an Inca king with a golden dick?" Did she actually say that out loud? And as if on cue, the sky suddenly let loose in torrents. Overturned soil couldn't absorb all the rain at once, and immediately began turning the dig into a muddy byre.

Raindrops slid over the sculpted planes of Blake's stern face. "There's that Inca king of your dream again. I'm flattered. But then I guess you know how many wives and concubines they had, not to mention how many children the average sire fathered." His gaze fell to her chest.

She crossed her arms over her nipples, poking obscenely through her sodden T-shirt. "And to think I was under the assumption you thought my dream was important."

"Oh, when you meet Roberto Diaz tomorrow morning, don't forget to mention that while you were supposedly out cold that first night, you called out to your king in the throes of an orgasm."

Rainwater streamed off the sagged brim of her hat, and she tossed it away. Now her hair was plastered to her head and she was soaked to her sunburned skin, but she was too angry to feel the cold as she stared wordlessly across the sieve at him.

"That's right," rainwater sputtered from his lips. "During your wet dream, you specifically evoked the name of king Atahualpa, in perfect English, I might add. And since no textbooks give his correct handle, which is *Virile Sweet One* , it looks as if this is another one of your unexplained phenomena." He crossed his arms. "Like not being able to speak Quechua," he added.

"But I *don't* know how to speak Quechua!" She was sputtering rainwater. "And I didn't know the meaning of his name. I always thought it meant *The Bird of Good Fortune!* I can't believe you actually think I faked a wet dream for your benefit. You're ridiculous!"

"I used to be ridiculous hoping for an assistant who would be willing to risk dysentery in a third world country, and just for the chance to piece together potsherds that may or may not answer an unsolved puzzle of the past."

The downpour she had prayed for earlier slowed to a light drizzle she blessed. Dark clouds passed, and Inti came out with an even hotter vengeance, causing steam to rise from the muddy ground. "So that's why you dropped your professorship. I can understand, but–"

"Do you actually think you were the first female to offer me her sexual favors to break into archaeology? When will you people realize the chance of discovering an un-robbed tomb is about a million to one?"

"Unless you've found Atahualpa's hidden ransom and are afraid I'll credit myself on the publication of your monumental discovery… my, God, you actually *have* found something, haven't you?"

"Now who's being absurd? Atahualpa's ransom is pure myth, nothing but stories told around the campfire by grandma and grandpa to a bunch of kids."

"But these people are the direct descendants of the Incas, you even said so yourself. Legends passed on from generation to generation are a viable key when it comes to unraveling the past. Especially since the Incas had no written language."

"You're right. Eating my own words gives me acute indigestion."

"So… are you?"

"Am I what?"

"On to something!"

"What I'm onto is this pre-Columbian garbage dump, not the kingly treasures of your kooky dreams. Jesus! Has anyone ever told you that you have a too vivid imagination? Aha, a boyfriend back in the hallowed halls of Stanford, perhaps?"

"You would've gotten along famously. J.J. Winslow lacked imagination, too."

"The old-money Winslow's? Very upper class for a small town girl from Kansas. I knew the father from my Harvard days. So tell me, is Junior as stuffed a shirt as the old man? Do I hear wedding bells in your future?"

"Why, Blake, if I didn't know better, I'd say you're jealous!"

"It must be the heat. It's gone to your head. You're imagining things again."

"And if you're imagining I slept my way to a PhD, you really have been holed up atop this mountain for too long. I broke my engagement with J.J. a year ago, not that it's any of your business." She sent the sieve flying.

He caught the wooden edge at his groin. "His loss."

"I'm also not some featherbrained student swept up in the silly hero worship you once inspired throughout the archeological community. Or are you deluded enough to believe I'd resort to the ridiculous ploys you accused me of just to garner your precious signature on my resume?"

"You're resume is impressive enough without my autograph." He swung the sieve back her way.

Her hands smacked flat down into the screen and she glared at him "That's right, Mud Head, so rest assured, I've no intention of seducing you to get an outstanding letter of recommendation from you at the end of this stint."

"You have to admit," he cocked an eyebrow, "your talented little show in the temple bath followed right on the heels of that sexy wet dream was a tad suspect."

"Oh? And did I fake passing out? Did I fake a nosebleed? Altitude sickness?" She clenched her fist and mud oozed up between her fingers. "Why, nobody could think more highly of you than you do, Doctor B.S."

"I know you didn't fake an orgasm with me, four to be exact," he growled, and then his eyes grew wide at the mud patty in her raised hand. "Don't even *think* about it."

She hit the bull's eye with a loud splat and immediately cupped a hand over her mouth, astonished by her own fury. "Oh…" She took a few steps back half afraid she would burst into laughter at the Mud Head picture he presented. His one muddy eye opened, and at his glowering expression, she spun around, making a mad, slippery dash for her only means of escape. But the second she reached for a rung on the ladder, and raised a mud-caked heel to step on it, he caught her by the ankle and flipped her over. She squawked, and landed face- down in mud.

"Pachamama's revenge," he laughed, watching as she struggled up onto her hands and knees in the muck.

Sitting upright, she swiped muck off her face, and opened her eyes to denim-encased tree trunk-like legs planted wide. She jacked her legs back, and they shot out.

The next thing he knew he was flat on his back, semi sunk in a squishy bog. His diggers laughed uproariously when the little witch used his chest as a doormat to make her getaway. He sat up just in time to see the ladder being pulled from her grasp, jerking its way up the high dirt wall.

"Hey! Put that back down this instant!" she yelled up at his men, and when they didn't comply, she stomped her boot in a puddle, spattering his face with more mud.

"*Amor serrano! Amor serrano!*" They shouted.

"In case you're interested, they're calling for "mountain-style love'." Blake hooked a finger into her back pocket, and yanked her off balance. She landed right where he wanted her, on her ass in the mud right beside him. "They're saying it's high time I took my woman in hand."

"What do you mean *your* woman?" Like cake at some bizarre wedding, she slapped his cheek with a handful of muck, and then frosted it around for good measure. "Macho pigs. Every last one of you," she grumbled to herself, and with elbows bent and braced on the backs of her hands, she disengaged her stuck bottom from the morass.

He gripped her arm, and she went sailing belly down across his thighs. "Unlike your politically correct Northern American gents," he said, locking his leg over her thighs, "Quechua machismo is not only correct here, but when it comes to you," he caught her one flaying hand and pinned her wrist at her back, "this is long overdue." He raised his hand.

Her tummy fluttered with dread, anticipation and wild confusion, as if her mind made some odd connection between arousal and his authoritative manner. "I guess it'll make you feel like a big man, beating a defenseless woman!"

"Defenseless!" He hooted without humor. "I can think of adjectives to describe you, but *defenseless* is not one of them. He lowered his hand, plans of a hearty smack to her bottom thwarted. "Damn. Maypez may have called you a *rupaq siki*, a phrase used to refer to a woman who is anxious to jump into bed with a man, but its literal translation means, 'hot rear end'. He reached under her belly, unsnapped and unzipped her pants. "Can't make your *siki* hot for all this mud clinging to the seat of your pants now, can I?"

"What are you doing! Stop that!" she shrieked as he hauled her pants down to her knees, exposing her bottom and sending off raucous male cheers from the lofty ring-side.

"Ah, now that's better," he announced, and her face burned with embarrassment. "Maypez was also correct about your *yuraq siki*, by the way. You do indeed have a very 'white ass', but not for long." His open hand flew down on her wet skin with the force of lightning and a loud crack like thunder.

"Yeoouch! Mother of God! That hurts!"

"It's supposed to…" He pelted her backside with fast strokes that set her flesh ablaze and stung like swarms of killer bees. "I should have done this the first day when you spied on me at the waterfall."

She lay across his lap panting with watering eyes, wanting him to stop the spanking, wanting it to go on; two opposing desires at war in her head. Her emotions whirled and skidded and her thundering heart coursed blood through her veins.

"I knew the first time I laid eyes on this perky bottom you were meant for this." Loud rifle shots resounded off her bouncy flesh, evoking a burning sweetness captive between her legs. Inti's inferno, could he see the creamy evidence between her pursed labial lips? Had she been waiting for this kind of sensuous sting all her life? His dominant mien, each determined smack he delivered, took her to a place which moved though her body so fast she couldn't return. Despite all her wild wiggling and yelps of protest, her mind took up a mantra of surrender... surrender... surrender...

He paused, massaging away the soreness and the sting. "You've been asking for this from day one, haven't you, little smartass? In fact, it looks as if you like this as much as I do." His bold announcement hit home worse than his hand striking her ass. It was true, although she would ice skate in hell before she admitted it to him. Even truer was his hard penis riding against her hip. His cock pulsed with the same beat that made her inner muscles spasm along with her stinging cheeks.

"Oh, please!" she hollered, not sure if she meant "please stop" or "please more". His finger took a torturous trace up and then down the crevice of her bottom, and she couldn't help relaxing her tightly clenched muscles.

"I won't stop until you to tell me what it is you're hoping for from me," he teased, and then suddenly, without warning, cracks ricocheted off one cheek to the next with dazzling speed, each one gaining in strength, each sting more intense than the last. She wondered how he knew her secrets, secrets she hardly knew about herself. Passion pounded through her heart, chest and brain, and her swollen clit and sodden vagina fairly throbbed, as hot and ready for his cock as her well-punished bottom.

"Oh, God," she moaned. "Just make love to me, Blake."

He delivered one last satisfying crack to her crimson bottom and gently gathered her sitting into his lap. Lost in the welling, jungle-green depths of her eyes, he inched his mouth closer to her lush lips. "By the way," he murmured, "all of your dreams are important to me, sweetheart."

His kiss was passionate and his warm tongue thrust into her mouth, which she opened submissively to his eager exploration. He skimmed a hand down her muddied back to her bare buttocks, giving her round mounds a possessive squeeze that made her mew against his mouth. His fierce intensity was meant to subdue her, but it only served to inflame her as she kissed him back with wild abandon.

Masculine shouts and sudden applause made him break their tongue battle to look up at the smiling Quechua faces.

Blake set her to the side and stood up. Mud cooled her hot bare *siki* while she jimmied into her sodden pants, twisted up around her thighs. Finished, she looked up at him with questioning eyes, and was reminded of the first time she ever saw him at the portal to the clouds in her sanctuary. He was again an aberration covered from hair-end to boot-tip in mud. Sunlight streamed around the black silhouette of his body, which had also blocked her from watchful eyes while she righted her pants. He bent to pluck up their backpacks, which he slung over his broad shoulder. When he offered her a helping hand, mottled and as red as she imagined her butt cheeks were at the moment, her heart skipped a fearful beat. She knew he would not be so gallant if he found out what she had hidden in her backpack. If he ever discovered that stolen artifact, she probably wouldn't be able to sit comfortably for a month of Sundays. His gritty palm felt as hot as her buttocks when she took it, and he pulled her to her feet. She loved tall men because they always made her keep her chin up.

He smiled warmly and, placing his large hand at the small of her back, escorted her to the ladder, which as if by magic had reappeared before her nose. Not wanting to face the diggers, she stared stubbornly at the rungs.

He pressed his erection tightly into her sore bottom, the fabric between them a frustrating barrier as shivers raced up the length of her spine. "Now," his whispering hot breath fanned her ear, and she felt him hook a finger into the rubber band holding her braid together. "Unless you want me to drag these muddy pants down again and hobble you…" a quick twist of his wrist snapped the band and lower hair coils spun free. "Unless you want me to fuck you right here with an audience, up you go."

"To where?" She was so aroused she was almost ready for him to take her from behind, right on the ladder, diggers be dammed.

"To that waterfall you saw off the beaten path, where you and I will come clean… together… like we should have weeks ago." He gave her *siki* a hearty smack that had her scaling the rungs in a hurry.

* * *

At the deep pool at the foot of the falls, Blake looked over Hope's shoulder, up into rainbows that arched through cascading waters that seemed as powerful as his desire for her. Mists through the rainbows, up to where the icy waters broke out of the tree line at the lip of a vast rock ledge hundreds of feet above, symbolized the spiritual beauty of the landscape. The roar of the falls was deafening... as if commanding mere mortals into silence.

Hope felt him move away, but she simply stared, transfixed in amazed wonder. Finally, she tore her eyes away and turned to see him hopping on one bare foot, prying free his boot. Giggling, she did the same, and then wiggled her weary toes into the spongy earth.

"You," he declared, sweeping her effortlessly up off her feet, "are a fucking mess!" And with that, he tossed her right into frigid water that stunned and revived her.

Long hair floating, mud rinsed away in the current, she emerged. Her toes touched bottom and she stood, waterline hip-level, hair slicked down her back to her butt. Her T-shirt clung to her tits, and like her pants, they were blessedly free of mud. She spun around, and saw him dive under the clear water. Muddied clouds bloomed behind him as he kicked his jean-clad legs.

He shot to the surface before her. Dark hair seal-slick and clean as well, droplets sparkling on his lashes and chest. He grinned like the devil himself, and then playfully plunked down his hand in a fanning splash that stung her face. His hazel eyes shone golden, challenging her to a race to the rock outcrop on the other side of the lagoon.

He touched rock first and surged out of the water. She had barely touched when he gripped her wrist, and pulled her up to join him under spray-off from the falls. They stood together on sun-warmed white granite partially covered by velvety looking moss. He was more heart-stopping than she imagined Adam would be in the misty rainbow paradise surrounding them. He reached for her waist, and yanked her

T-shirt up and off. Her arms came down, and her breasts settled with a jiggle, hard nipples dusky pink and standing at attention. He caught and held her gaze while he unzipped his jeans and drew out his erection. Despite the cold spray, his heavily veined penis sprouted from the open placket of his sodden jeans, the head enormously swollen, like a lusciously ripe, dew-kissed plum.

"Oh, my!" she gasped and felt a rush of liquid heat that had her squeezing her thighs together. She wanted to fall to her knees and take him in her mouth, run her worshiping tongue around his head, and slide his long length into the tunnel of her throat. She peeked at him, suddenly shy.

He smiled as if he knew exactly what she was thinking, pushed his pants down, and kicked them off. He placed his hands on her shoulders and pressed down.

Loving the unabashed dominance in him, she knelt in soft moss between his naked thighs.

His palm cupped her chin, raising it to his assessing gaze probing the very depths of her soul. "Now you can finish what I started in your sanctuary that first night." His tone was low and uncompromising, but also thrilling in that he was claiming her. "Stop me if I'm wrong, Hope, but this power trip makes you hot."

She nodded in silent assent, and then clutched his knees for support, taking in all that made him male. His masculine musk intoxicated her; the site of his proud, stiff manhood and furry sacks exciting her unbearably. He wound his fingers through her hair and milked his cock until the tip cried for her attention. Cupping his testicles gently, she firmly gripped his enormous cock, lowering it to just before her lips, giving him a teasing stroke. She felt him tighten his fist in her hair, and she obediently licked the single pearly droplet, relishing the salty essence of him, and then kissing the crown.

He stopped her hungry ministrations abruptly, his cock popping free from her mouth as he pulled her to her feet. He bent down, and she held onto his shoulder while he peeled her wet pants and panties down to her ankles. Once she stepped out of the sodden tangle, he straightened up, and it was as if he were photographing every inch of her naked body with his eyes.

"More beautiful than in the temple bath," he pronounced, and hauled her naked body to his warm solid chest, rotating his hips and grinding his hard, hot cock against her soft tummy. "Tell me how much you want me inside you, sweet Hope-of-High-Hopes. I need to hear you say it." His lips captured hers and his knee parted her thighs. Thrusting two fingers inside her ready pussy, he moved his thumb over her slick clit in slow, sensual circles. Her knees buckled and they tumbled, she onto her back on the moss, he onto his side, where he commenced devouring her with kisses.

She lifted her ample breasts in her hands, offering them up to him, accentuating their lushness. He caught a nipple in his mouth, nipping it with his teeth, sucking the areola hungrily. His tongue worked feverish circles over her hard nipple, his fingers skimming her belly to her groin, combing her auburn bush, feeling her crisp curls dampen with her love juices. Her one breast slipped free of his ravenous mouth, and her saliva–slick nipple slipped past his cheek. His tongue flicked like a serpent's into her navel, then moved down through a fragrant moss more sweet and natural than the bed beneath. He forced her legs wider, and he buried his face in her pussy. Licking and probing, his demanding tongue explored every creamy crevice.

Digging Up Destiny

Hope moaned and thrashed her head, her hair a cloud of fire. His tongue stabbed at her clit, lapping greedily, reveling in her salty taste. She reached for his cock, but he smacked her hand away, intent on tasting her surrender to the full. And when she was on the verge of screaming, he rose up to kneel between her thighs, gripped his cock, and placed its potent length at the threshold of his true home.

"Tell me what it is that you want. Beg me for it," he demanded, teasing her unmercifully with the tip of his manhood, slipping in and out just ahead of her clutching pussy lips. He chuckled at her cries of frustration as she closed her legs around his waist.

Hands on his hips, she pressed him down, and in. "Oh, Please, oh, God, fuck me, now, before I go mad!"

Plunging into her at last, he wondered why he had waited so long for this heaven. Her hips rose to meet his, and then fell away, their urgent rhythms quickly meshing. He thrust deeply and slowly inward, then pulled out again, driving each thrust a little faster, flesh slapping against flesh. Her breaths quickened while he ground her sore bottom into the cool moss, and soon she was gasping for air. Hungry sucking of her juices accompanied his hard ride while she clamped her legs tighter around him. Her inner muscles clutched at his cock, enfolding it, reluctant to let go, then opening to greet each new penetration, and once again refusing to give him up easily. She chewed at the back of one closed fist, trying to muffle the sound of her cries. She broke off with a choking sob, and he felt himself explode inside her. She went limp beneath him, but refused to let him withdraw.

"Stay there... stay right there," she begged. "Don't go. I'll feel so empty if you do."

He let his weight down gently, supporting himself on his elbows. He stared into her face, seeing himself reflected in the jungle-green pools of her irises. "Why are you crying?" he whispered, concerned, twisting his fingers into her hair, the same fiery red as her sexy snatch. "Surely not from the spanking? Turn over and let's have a look at that shapely *siki* so I can kiss it better."

"You know full well I liked and loathed every minute of that!" She laughed.

"Kinky girl that you are. Would you like me to re-heat it?"

"No! My poor *siki's* still sore."

"Then you had best tell me the reason for the waterworks or it'll be sorer still," he warned.

She swiped her eyes dry. "I cried because I was happy, okay, already?" She wrapped her arms around his neck. "Promise me something?" she ventured, tightening her cunt playfully, tugging at his slowly shrinking erection, teasing it back to attention.

"Anything!" he breathed, feeling himself stir deep inside her where he wanted to stay forever, it seemed. He began to grind his hips in slow circles. "What is it that you want?" he teased her back.

"Let me in on your secret… whatever that is. Don't send me off to the village tomorrow with Roberto Diaz."

His eyes flashed pain, quickly replaced by fury "I thought you were different." He slipped out of her, and she did indeed feel empty, as if her life-force had been frozen and her heart ceased functioning. "And I played into it like a dammed fool."

"Played into what? What do you mean?"

"I guess I'm not the first guy to be led around by his cock." He jerked his legs into his jeans, and zipped them closed. "Get dressed," he said thickly. "The party's over."

Digging Up Destiny

"What did I say? Please, Blake, I don't understand."

"As I said, you weren't the first female to offer me her sexual favors for a favor in return. Although your methods of seduction were, admittedly, the most inventive, masturbating in the temple bath, orgasmic dreams with kings, speaking in tongues. But today was truly the most enjoyable performance."

Chapter Six

Dressed in full hiking gear, Hope stood beside the famous Inca sundial the *Intihuatana* atop one of the highest plazas within the Lost City of the Clouds. She watched the huge orange ball of the sun began to rise between the V of two lush green mountain peaks, and wiped away the last of her tears. She closed her eyes, feeling the healing warmth caress her face and the red fill her field of vision, penetrating her eyelids with blood-filtered light. She kept her eyes closed and took a deep, reinforcing breath of the charged thin air, held it for a ten count, and exhaled slowly, cleansing her mind and soul of thoughts of Blake. At the sound of heavy footsteps coming up behind, her heart instantly betrayed her, bumping in hopeful anticipation.

"When the Sun shed a tear that landed on the Earth, the Sun gave his children a token of what they would become," Alex said in his gentle baritone, and she turned to face him. "The *Intihuatana*. *Inti* means sun and hata means to tie and *Intihuatana* is translated as 'The Hitching Post of the Sun'. It's an intriguing architectural masterpiece, isn't it? The Inca had no knowledge of the wheel, yet they sculpted these geometric planes and angles from single blocks of white granite throughout the four corners of their empire. The Spaniards lopped off the tops of off most of these holy Inca stones, so it's rare to find one intact. It's comforting to know a place of such spiritual beauty and wonder never knew the kick of a conquistador's boot. Only eighty miles from the captured capital of Cuzco, and the mountains hid this scared city so well the greedy gold suckers never knew it was here. It's enough to make one a believer in the protective spirit of the mountains, the power of the Apus. Ah, but I'm rambling again like a doddering professor. My apologies. I came to tell you the shaman, Roberto Diaz, has arrived, and will wait for you at the Pachamama Stone."

"Just like my arrival to Machu Picchu... Blake didn't come to greet me then... or to see me off now. He sent his architect friend."

"He's in love with you, too, Hope, he just doesn't know it because the idiot actually thinks we have no idea he's onto something. And whatever he's found, it's got to be of huge historical significance for him to keep it from either you or me."

"Me I can almost understand. But you, Alex?" she scoffed. "The way he worries about your bad heart in this altitude, reminding you to take your medicine, he's like an old mother hen."

"I should put my pills in my cereal bowel, pour milk over them, and call it the Breakfast of Champions. This is more likely than not another reason for Blake's not divulging what he's onto. On top of which, I have orders to retire my shovel and any sort of heavy labor in a dig, and I don't take well to orders."

"I understand you two have been stuck together throughout the course of his career."

"Longer than that. Blake's father and mother were Egyptologists. His mother, Lori... in some ways you remind me a little of her... she was a dear friend to the brash young man I was at the time, to all of us on that cursed expedition. I later came to think of the project as the 'horrible obsession' that destroyed Joe Sevenson. And Lori… she paid the highest price, being married to him. The Valley of the Kings is nothing but rock gorges that can flood in a simple rain storm and fill like a bathtub in a matter of minutes. It was heaven for a young boy and hell on his mother when Blake went off alone on one of his infamous explorations. And that was more often than not. His father had little enough patience and couldn't abide having Blake underfoot. And that turned out to be a blessing in disguise. The crane was at the top of the ravine, lifting out the stone. I looked up and saw the chains weren't distributing the weight evenly. I was safest at the bottom, but the Sevenson's were on the gorge directly across and above me. I knew if the top chain blew that the rock would land on them. I red-flagged the crane operator to back up and to pull left, but it was too late."

"Oh, dear God, no!"

"*Nothing* was worse than when I found Blake in a small cave directly behind the whole scene. He just stared and rocked. God only knows what the little mite saw or what the grown man still remembers."

Hope's eyes filled for the little boy unable to comprehend the horror, not wanting to, but at the same time trying to understand.

"When I carried him to my truck, the only thing Blake said was, 'I'm sorry I played hide and seek, Alex.'"

"What became of him after that?"

"I know, only too well, when you have no blood relative left in the world, you can feel as if you're starting to disappear. But the dammed adoption agency said I traveled too much. I was also single, and that was taboo back then. I never did marry. I guess I never stayed in one place long enough to have a lady fall in love with me."

Even with his snow-white hair, gravity-etched face, and barely discernable paunch, Alex was still a handsome man. Hope imagined the younger version must have been stunning. "I find that hard to believe Mister Neville. I 'm quite smitten with you."

"You're making an old man blush and I love you for it."

"What became of Blake when you couldn't adopt?"

"I can't imagine them trekking up Machu Picchu to handcuff me for kidnapping a forty-two year old man," he laughed. "And he had quite an education roaming the world with me and his private tutor, Mr. Rubin. Blake wanted to continue his parents' work so their deaths weren't in vain, but he didn't want to leave me. In the end I shipped him off to Harvard."

"How did he take having the wind knocked out of his sails?"

Alex chuckled in remembrance. "He returned all my letters and wouldn't accept my calls

for two weeks. Anyway, years later he thanked me. I was standing on a tarmac shaking Doctor B.S.'s hand. I suspect he taught the professors a thing or two. He spoke seven languages before he left this old bag of bones."

"You've been a better father to him than any ten adoption agencies would have found him!"

"Well that remains to be seen. And if he knows what's good for him, he'll ask you to marry him and not turn into a lonely old windbag like me."

Hope hugged him and mentally struggled to lighten his mood. "If he asked me, Alex, I would never accept. You see, I'm too in love with you. Odds are too stacked against him. What man could ever win me over with your sort of competition?"

"Hmm." He rubbed her back. "Damned right." He broke his hold. "But I fear with Blake the apple doesn't fall far from the tree. I'm afraid he's as obsessed with his mysterious find as his father was with his project. It may take an act of God, but I have faith that he has enough of me in him that he'll come to his senses. Don't give up on him yet, my dear girl."

She kissed his cheek, and noticing a satchel by his boot, she changed the subject. "What's that, you dear man, a present for me?"

"Actually, its requisite tokens to give when you meet a master shaman. A bottle of *pisco* from Maypez, also a drawstring pouch filled with sacred coca leaves handpicked by her. Oh, and Maypez told me to tell you something she felt was of utmost importance, but dammed if I understand it. She must have fifteen years on me, but she seems quite smitten by this young handsome shaman. She said to tell you that Roberto Diaz is the master shaman of dreams. That he's made them come true for many a young girl, especially those who suffer from a broken heart."

* * *

I am honored, Hope Burnsmyre, that you chose me, master shaman, *hatun laika*, don Roberto Diaz, to share the details of your dream. I will gladly interpret it in the ancient ways of my ancestors." He bent to kiss her hand. Blue-black hair fell forward in two silky looking sheets while he held her gaze with soft brown, compellingly beautiful Inca eyes. His skin was swarthy, his nose long and slightly hooked at the tip, cheekbones wide and high like his proud forehead. "Freud knew most dreams were of a sexual nature, and your dream of king Atahualpa is clearly such." He straightened, dressed in a red vicuña poncho, black trousers, and leather sandals. Short and stocky like his ancestors, he was a mere head taller than her, and Hope agreed with Maypez – Roberto Diaz did indeed have a presence that would make Quechua maids and maidens swoon under his magnetic spell.

"The pleasure is mine, *Maestro*." She addresses him as 'master', which she knew was the proper title of respect given to a shaman.

"But please, *Mamacona*, you must call me Roberto. I insist!"

Hope blushed at being referred to as his initiate. "For you... Roberto." She handed him the requisite gifts. "These are from Maypez, who speaks highly of you."

"There has never been a more loving and generous heart than my dream girl, Maypez. And you must also tell Alexander I would like to journey with him as well."

"I'm sure he will look forward to it as much as I am looking forward to my journey with you today."

"Yet it will be difficult, for you must shed your western psychology that teaches you to reconcile yourself with the past, with your mother and father and your history. To embrace our esoteric ways and learn to reconcile you with the future is not easy. You must craft your own destiny; become a steward of the world that you wish our children to inherit. The way of the visionary is to assume responsibility for who we are becoming – to influence destiny by envisioning the possible and leading it across the dance floor. You must accept the unexpected," he patted her hand and let go, "for the unexpected will be redefined with me." He smiled a warm show of square white teeth with a charming slight space between them that made her smile and relax in his company.

In fact, she had never felt so relaxed around anyone in her entire life. She shrugged on her backpack, and signaled thumbs up – ready, prepared, and able to follow wherever he would lead.

He pointed to the dark, shadowy mountain always present in the backdrop of the famed photographs of Machu Picchu's ruins. "We will scale Huayna Picchu and visit The Temple of the Moon!" His excited, classic Inca face then became solemn as he took three coca leaves from the pouch, and facing the sun raised his hand and chanted a prayer in a beautiful singing voice, letting the wind take his offering.

Hope gazed up with respect at the enormous peak as she started down the trail behind him. Bromides clung to black rockslides in little splashes of reds and yellows down to the surrounding, lush green valley. Roberto's hair blew around his shoulders in the warm breeze as they made their way down the zigzagging path, and then arrived at the top of a flight of twelve stone steps carved by the Inca. Below were two stone trails flanked by dry aqueducts. One path veered to the left, the other to the right.

"This stairway marks an energy line," he said, pointing to the right. "This way is a structured, mystical path, a spiritual way to Viracocha or whatever name you use for the creator. To the left is the magical and practical application of the power you receive as *Mamacona*, once you have followed the right-hand path. And this you have already done, perhaps without knowing, on your first journey to Machu Picchu. The left-hand path is wilder, and it can be chaotic. We shall go this way." He stepped down. "And now that you have paid homage and have mingled your tears with Inti, we will visit Mama Killya, mother moon, before his sweat and tears and her own can be revealed."

Hope froze in her tracks. How could he possibly know she had been crying at The Hitching Post of the Sun when he wasn't there?

"In your dream, the one who both pursued and led you on the Inca trails is here. And just as you dreamed it, we must go up in order to go back to the place of origin. The faceless stranger is no longer faceless."

"Roberto, what do you mean?"

"Ah!" He waved off her fear as if it were a bothersome fly. "A month ago, in the Amazon, I partook of the Vine of Life. I dreamed the same dream you dreamed. I saw you in a vision, a red-haired *Mamacona*. You were lost and traveling on the Inca trails, but you could not see me. I was the faceless stranger showing you the way to Machu Picchu, showing you the path to your future. In my vision, I saw Altahulpa implant his secret within you for safekeeping."

"But how can this be?"

"With both of us dreaming the same thing, how can it not be true? The energy created by our dreaming is like the air, it travels everywhere." He looked into her eyes, and she felt he was gazing into the depths of her soul. His eyes were like magnets. "Your ability to use this energy is limited only by your dream of its power, by your faith. Our dreams can affect everyone and everything else if we energize them with enough power." He searched her eyes. "Do you believe this, Hope?"

"Yes. In my culture, they say to be careful of the friends you keep because one person's energy rubs off on another. One bad apple spoils the whole good bunch of apples. If you hang out with negative people, you'll become negative yourself. On the other hand, a confident leader inspires confidence."

"So the ways we are taught to dream are not that different at all."

"Well, actually, they are extremely different."

"Daydreams, night dreams," he waved. "Anyone can be a shaman. And you don't need The Vine of Life to do so, although partaking can open the hard, stubborn place that closed when you were born of your mother. Right here," he touched her head, referring to the soft spot on babies. "To know the images, voices, smells, feelings, and tastes that inhabit the inner recesses of body and soul is to understand that dreaming is not restricted to the hours we sleep. And when we honor our dreams, we empower ourselves. It is not as difficult as you think to tap into the knowledge of that spirit put into everyone. Writers, poets, artists, they do it all the time, do they not, sweet Hope-of-High-Hopes?"

She gasped. "But how did you know Blake calls me that? Did he tell you?"

"You carry a lot of heavy energy in your aura that the lovesick do. There are dark spots at your chakras... here," he ran his hand over her heart, "and here" then over her tummy. "But there is also much good energy between the two of you left here," he swirled his hand just above her mons, and it fairly sizzled. His hand came away and he winked. "Shamans are not celibate you know." The endearing gap between his teeth actually made her laugh, and she didn't know if it was because she was entirely freaked out or because he made absolute sense.

"To me sex is a joy,' he went on. 'Yet I fast and refrain from sex before I *camay* or heal a person with trapped or heavy energy. To those unfortunate enough to harbor sexual anxieties, I tell them to try and find something sexually attractive about nearly everyone as it exercises the erogenous zone in your brain. Sometimes the only way to get on higher ground is to climb, as we are doing now. It makes the heart pump faster and you grow excited the closer you get to the summit."

And the hill they scaled made her out of breath in the thin air, as if she were climbing a stair-master to the sky. "Yeah, well, I had a fiancé who you could *camay* till doomsday and you couldn't clear up his issues."

"Sexual anxiety is stirred by our fears of entrapment, our conflicts with dependency, and identity, as much as it's stirred over the sex act itself."

"Now I have a lover who's great in bed, but he has trust issues and he's obsessed with... something." She was slipping on loose rocks on the steep climb.

"Obsession is heavy energy, as is greed, which the Spanish had for gold. Love is the purest, most refined energy. It conquers all obstacles. Sexual energy is both refined and heavy energy. Depending on your partner and whether or not the energy balances, this balancing is also like a seesaw. Pursuit is a seesaw, with two people inching forward, and then pulling back. Like the sexual act itself. How much does he care? How serious is he? These are the questions most women ask. The simple answer is an endurance test. You want to find out if you come first with him."

They made it to the top of the grade, and climbed onto a grassy terrace where the Inca once cultivated medicinal plants.

"Jealousy tests work just as well, *Mamacona*." His eyes locked onto hers and he flipped his poncho back over his shoulders, stepped closer, and raised his hand palm up facing her, inviting her to touch it." Risk becoming lovers with me."

Excitement coiled in her tummy. Roberto's eyes were expectant, quietly waiting. Her gaze left his to his upraised hand. She gasped at the deep purple scar that ran across his lifeline, down his wrist, and clear up to his elbow, disappearing under the red fold of his poncho. The stories were true. Roberto had been struck by lighting and was alive and well and standing before her. Her blood was roaring in her ears now and her breath was coming shallowly. His eyes beckoned her, steady and reassuring. She lifted her hand, and it was trembling. Slowly, she brought it close to his, and then palm to palm.

There was an explosion of blue–white light, rushing warmth and electrifying sensations. She forgot to breathe. She no longer felt her heart beating; her body was a flashing magnetic bombardment of sensations, a kaleidoscope of colors, a whooshing rush in her ears, the taste of something achingly sweet on her tongue, and Roberto... he permeated her, washed through her with light and liquid heat, charging electrons, rearranging atoms and cells until she was not only touching him, but for a brief, illusive minute was part of him. She was as inside his thoughts as he was hers. She knew, tasted, felt, became a part of everything he had known or had ever been. Great joy, terrible sorrow, yearning, celebration, wonder, explosive elation and quiet serenity were hers, and they were his, and there was no seam at the joining.

And then abruptly it was over, Roberto stepped back, and his hand came away. Hope was frozen. Every nerve in her body tingled. Her limbs were wobbly with a function she couldn't recall. She gradually realized the sound she heard was the expulsion of her own breath, and she was disoriented as if the altitude had gotten to her again, but at the same time, she was filled with arousal, with a need so intense she felt her body would spontaneous combust, leaving a pile of smoldering ash on the grass if he merely kissed her.

She opened her clenched fist, and stared at a polished oval river stone that was rather nondescript except for the marbleized veins of blue and purple, touches of yellow, and swirls of red, embedded in it. A thousand things ached in throat with a need to express them, but all she could manage to mutter was, "You've given me a gift, Maestro."

"It's *khuya* . Meditate alone and listen to it someday. It has many stories for you to hear that it has witnessed in its long existence. But as far as it being a gift, it is *you* who have given the *gift* to me. I could never possess this power if not for the collective love for pachamama, and the combined power of dreams. Your wish was to become 'one with the universe' was it not, Mamacona?"

She nodded.

"Is that a *no*?" He looked closely at her face. "Or a *yes*?"

"A yes!"

"Very good!" He slipped his poncho off his head and the shiny length of his hair tumbled over his bare shoulders and chest like condor wings. He began to whip the red cloth around his head like a matador, at first slowly, and then gaining speed; faster and faster and faster he twirled it, until it was a red blur of satin, ermine, velvet, silk, and then fire swirling in a descending fury, a flashing tornado of desire twisting down and around her body, whipping up from her toes to her head, tingling like thousands of butterflies fluttering over her flesh. She felt the collective consciousness of infinite lovers in strobes of pressure on her lips, as wet flicks on her breasts, and as exquisite penetrations of invisible fingers in her vagina – full body bombardments of amazing foreplay in the space of mere seconds that stole her breath away. Then he let go and the red poncho wafted down from the air. She could see handprints, and somehow knew it was the *Apus* smoothing out wrinkles until the fabric was a perfect picnic blanket on the soft grass. Hope looked down at herself. She was naked! Her incredulous gaze shot across to Roberto. He was completely naked, too, and on the wall behind him rested their sandals, boots, backpack, and clothes.

Before she could so much as blink, he spun on one heel, his proud cock swinging round and out of view, and fell back across the blanket. With a slight bounce, red rose petals flew up into the air and then down, landing on his hairless body in key places that had her mouth watering.

Laughing at his Pan-like antics, Hope joined him, bouncing on the luxuriant suppleness, rose petals settling on her breasts and vulva in a fragrant caress. Beneath his probing gaze, Inti's soft summer rays emanated from the dark moons of his pupils, radiating healing warmth into every cell of body.

His hand hovered over one of her rose-covered breasts, swirling in smoky circles above her flesh, red petals rising one by one collecting on his palm like metal responding to a magnet and subjecting her to the most utterly exquisite sensations. Quick tugs of a warm, wet mouth, fast wet licks of a lover's teasing tongue, and that magical hand skimmed above the shimmering horizon of her torso and belly, becoming a sizzling swirl over her navel before moving down farther. Her public hairs rose in a static, electrifying charge, cracking pinpoint sparks beneath his lightning-hot palm. Her pussy flowed with molten juices, her quivering legs opened wide, her hips seeking, reaching, her labia blooming open like a nested baby bird's mouth hungering for a lusty meal. Roberto's lips were suddenly there just above the creamy seam, blowing softy, ruffling her pubic hairs in a warm and feathery stream of blue-white breath. She moaned softly, and the sound traveled throughout the mountains. Sensually rich and deeply protective, the *Apus* joined in with strangely haunting melodies, barely audible, like a breeze... or was it the lull of ocean waves?

Digging Up Destiny

The sea! She could smell it. And coconuts; her sun-washed skin was suddenly slick with the oily essence of coconut. She could feel sand, soft as silk, beneath her. Like a film shot in soft focus, edges blurred as he rose above her. She raised her arms, embracing the shape of his lean, muscled back, threading the wealth of his hair though her fingers, feeling a familiar heat and texture, the oiled, sun-kissed skin beneath her palms. She tasted the warm hollow of his neck and inhaled the scent of him she could never define... the sea, the jungle, sandalwood, snow, rain, earth... it changed like the seasons.

She felt the pressure of his thighs, strong and muscled, against hers, and then they fit together like rain in the springtime, his penis entering her wet, snug warmth in a gentle wave before the surf rushed over them and he became a hot tide crashing forcefully between the open shore of her legs, his body rocking over hers thrusting harder and faster. An incredible feeling of love enveloped her. A vow too wrought with emotion to leave her lips was expressed in tender kisses, in fierce kisses, in kisses that tasted like more, always more than a mortal joining. They shattered into a million glowing stars, became one in an explosive culmination, setting the world spinning on its axis...

Hope opened her drowsy eyes. It was night and she was lying on the grass beneath the stars, looking up at the full moon. Her stomach felt full. Favorite tastes lingered faintly on her tongue... filet mignon, lemony asparagus, succulent strawberries, and chocolate. She was fully dressed. Roberto was also dressed and sitting crossed-legged beside her beside a crackling campfire. He was laying out an offering to Pachamama, several offerings from three ecological regions – three coca leaves to represent the sun, moon, and earth of the Inca trinity, a seashell jungle and mountaintop *khuays*, and grains of multicolored corn like jewels from the valley.

"We should meditate now, Hope, and pray for our families, our loved ones, for anything we want to." He chanted Quechua prayers in his beautiful voice, and after a time carefully wrapped all the offerings in paper, tied it closed with string, asked permission to live on the land, and tossed it into the fire.

They watched the smoke travel up towards the moon. Utter calm had seeped into her soul, a sense of peace in which everything was right with the universe, making the many questions she might have asked about their coupling feel unnecessary.

Roberto reclined on his side, and titled the bottle of *pisco* to his lips, offering her a taste, which she declined. He smiled at her. "I told you there was much good energy between the two of you. Your man… he has amazing sexual fantasies about you."

Her eyes grew wide. "Those were Blake's fantasies when we were…"

"Merely one of many. Yes."

Peace be dammed! She grabbed the bottle out of his hand and took a big, fortifying swig. Immediately, she spewed out two-hundred proof liquid into the campfire in a whooshing, dragon- breath ignition.

"That is one way to release heavy energy, mamacona!" Roberto exclaimed in delight, laughing and pounding her on the back while she coughed and dragged in a draft of air.

"What *else* do you know?" She wiped her mouth, her eyes still watering

"He is a sensualist and a naturalist, a wonderfully kinky alpha man of diverse tastes who, like you, harbors no heavy sexual anxieties or inhibitions."

Digging Up Destiny

"Why won't he share his secret with me?"

"Heavy obsession inherited from the biological father along with the death of his parents weighs down the lighter, refined energies of his trust and love, clouding his reasoning. Lack of sleep compounds it. He spends each night digging for the missing sunburst hidden in your rucksack. Or he digs in vain under the Inca-built wall barricading The Cave of Tears. He leaves, near to tears of frustration himself, because he can't get into Pachamama's womb. She has frozen him out like a frigid woman. And Atahualpa scares him with the curse of a king. At the waterfall before each dawn, Doc washes the muddy evidence off his clothes, lays them out on the rocks to dry, spreads out naked beside them and Inti warms and dries him at sunrise. But that's not the only thing that rises! He cannot sleep for dreaming of you, Sweet Hope-of-High-Hopes. After cursing you, he takes himself in hand and dreams of making love to you until he climaxes. There was that one instance when-"

"Stop! I've heard enough!" She made another grab for the bottle and this time had no problem swallowing a generous mouthful.

"My time with you is nearly over, Mamacona," he declared sadly.

"W-what do you mean?" Her heart tightened in her chest.

"Since time began, for every woman there is a man and for every man a woman he is destined to love." The whisper of a kiss brushed her hair, and she realized they were standing inside The Temple of the Moon at the summit of the mountain.

He stretched out his hand as if beckoning to the full moon. "But see how my wife sheds sorrowful silver tears for me? Yet the *Apus* knows I love every last one in all their infinite variety." He turned to her and smiled into her eyes. "Doc told you that *Pachacuti* means 'earth' or 'time'. *Pacha* 'to set

things right', '*cuti*',' time to set things right'. It is time to set things right."
He raised his hand to her, and just as before, she raised hers, only it wasn't trembling this time as she placed it against his, palm to palm.

There was a brilliant flash of silver-white light, and he appeared in a gold crown with red plumes and gold discs hanging from his earlobes. Small in stature, but powerfully proportioned, and she took him all in ravenously – his broad, hairless chest, his lean torso, his proud erection and imperial ingots at the apex of his sturdy thighs dusted in pulverized gold. "You are the chosen one, Hope, the keeper of the half. Return what has been lost to the Temple of the Sun, humble servant of Viracocha, so that all the human Children of the Sun may see the greatness that once ruled in Cuzco, the capital of my empire, the navel of Pachamama. What is past is past, and it should no longer be hidden." He became a sun god sculpted from pure bullion, not flesh and blood at all, and his touch went cold and began to fade; she could no longer feel him. She tried to cry out to him, but she had no voice. She could feel him slipping away. "The one who digs has remembered the meaning of *waylluy*. Go to him now." There was only a faint, shimmering outline of the golden splendor he had once been, a fading memory marching across time. "*Munaway wiñaypaq!*"

Hope found her voice, "Virile Sweet One!" She stumbled forward, reaching for him, but her fingers grasped only air.

* * *

Blake took steps two at a time, coming up onto an Inca lookout post that granted him a panoramic view of the deep valley, the thundering river below, and the towering mountains that surrounded the ancient ruins of Machu Picchu.

Digging Up Destiny

"You look like an imperial Inca soldier watching for Pizarro's army," Alex commented, making his presence known. He then bent his snowy head to binoculars mounted on a tripod. His skin crinkled around the eyepiece as he adjusted magnifications, viewing Huayna Picchu's mountainous terrain dotted with ancient trails, stairs, tunnels, terraces, precipitous slopes, and structures carved into sheer cliffs to the summit which housed The Temple of the Moon. "Shouldn't you be busy with something? Or did you decide to take the day off for a little site seeing?"

Hands locked behind his back, Blake began pacing. "I wonder… why didn't you ever marry, Alex? I remember growing up with you. I can name a list of shapely aunts the length of my arm."

"And what in God's name would make you bring that up?"

Blake grumbled something unintelligible.

"Got something on your mind, son?"

"Huh?"

Alex turned to face him. "You're about to succeed, where centuries could not, in wearing a path right into this granite plaza! Now spit it out!"

"I've been to the entrance gate of Huayna Picchu. The fool guard has no signatures in his book register under either Hope or Diaz's names."

"So he was probably taking a siesta when they passed through and they didn't want to wake him. It happens all the time."

"But they're not down from the mountain yet."

"They haven't been gone all that long."

"But it smells like rain. Those trails are slippery when wet. And there are the mud slides. Do you know how many people have fallen and seriously injured or killed each year?"

"Diaz is a native who scales ice mountains. And Hope has move than proven herself on the trek here, and carried her weight. As I recall, it took you four days in Cuzco to acclimatize before we arrived."

"You're right. I'm overreacting, I guess."

"You *guess*?"

Blake commenced pacing. "I was just thinking…"

"Perish the thought." Alex lowered his head to the binoculars again.

"I mean… what do we *really* know about this shaman?"

"Roberto Diaz is a fifth level Qero shaman highly recommended by Maypez. That tells me all a need to know."

"But Hope's so curious about everything. She's innocent, in some ways, and much too trusting."

"I agree."

"So what if this guy's a *bruja*?"

"An evil witchdoctor that uses black magic to prey on the vulnerable? Surely you jest."

"Why, the bastard could be taking advantage of her right now, as we speak! Doctoring her Gatorade, seducing her while she's on some psychotropic potion!"

"For crying out loud, Blake, Maypez called him the master shaman of dreams and said he's made them come true for many a girl, especially those who suffer from a broken heart. You could hardly call a healer of the lovelorn a *bruja*."

"And that's supposed to make me feel better? Damn it, Alex, you know I'm in love with her, so much so that I can't think straight."

"Then why don't you tell her, you ass?"

"Can you see them in that fucking thing yet? Are they coming down?"

Digging Up Destiny

"Machu Picchu translated means 'Old Peak'. That's exactly what I feel like doing this, an old peek. Here, be my guest." Alex invited him to use his equipment.

Blake almost knocked it over. "I just know something's wrong. I can feel it."

"Hallo! Hallo!" A woman's accented voice rang out like a fork to fine crystal, and then she appeared, rising up from the Inca stairway, first a mature, exotic face with silver-streaked, black hair tied up in a loose bun sporting a red rose, then a black-flounced blouse that showcased mouth-watering bosoms, and an hourglass figure moving towards them gracefully, but with enough hip sway to pull her Spanish-style skirt in alternate directions. "I'm so lost!" She laughed nervously. "I wonder if you can help me." She handed Alex a tourist map of the ruins. "I must find the Pachamama Stone. I'm supposed to meet someone there. And I'm so afraid I'll be late."

Alex was drawn into the most amazingly green feline eyes he ever had the pleasure to behold. "Why of course, *Señorita*. And your name is?" He cocked his ear close, inhaling the subtly intoxicating sent of her rose, and something else he couldn't quite put his finger on.

She smiled an absolutely enchanting show of tiny keyboard teeth set between dulcet lips. "Roberta Diaz. And you?"

Alex dragged his stare away, looking for Blake, who was long gone down the adjacent stone steps, headed for Hope and the entrance to Huayna Picchu.

Chapter Seven

Blake swung around the Pachamama Stone, and looking over tourist's heads lined up at the gate, he collided right into Hope spinning out of the exit.

"Still don't know whether your coming or going, Mud Head?"

"Are you all right?" He ran his hands up and down her body as if checking for broken bones. "Where is that *bruja* bastard? I'll kill him if he touched you."

"God, will you calm down! What *bruja* bastard?"

"Roberto Diaz," he said, still out of breath from running.

"He never showed up, so I went on the tour up the mountain."

"By yourself?"

"Yes, by myself. Why?"

"Diaz isn't a man. The shaman is a *she*, a woman by the name of Roberta who is looking for you, by the way." Blake glanced over his shoulder as if the hounds of hell were hot on his heels.

"But Maypez said Diaz was a man."

"Male or female, I've had it with shamans of any gender, I tell you. Come on let's get the hell out of here." He pulled her along by her hand into the Enigmatic Window, out the other side of the temple, and across the courtyard.

"But I want to meet her!" Hope locked her legs and skidded across the granite until he stopped. "I fell asleep in the Temple of the Moon and I had these dreams about the shaman and the king I want to ask her about."

"Fuck your dreams!"

"Well, now that you mention it, there *was* a lot of that going on."

He scrubbed at his face. "Jesus. I'm sorry. I'm stir crazy. I didn't mean that. Your dreams are my dreams."

"That's what I wanted to tell you before you before I was so rudely interrupted"

"I fell asleep on the rocks by the waterfall, Hope. I dreamed you were up that mountain doing things that made me crazy."

"Really? Like what?"

"Like this." He grabbed her freckled face between his hands and planted a hard, fast kiss on her lips that rocked her on her feet before he let go. "And this." He swept her off her feet and carried her through the halls, past the temple baths and her sanctuary, and the fountains, and the gardens, right into the jungle where he finally set her down.

"Want to compare notes on our dreams?" She walked beside him on the Inca trail.

"No."

"Come on. Just one question can't hurt"

"Arguing with you is like trying to blow out a light bulb!"

"Did you fantasize about rose petals and us on the beach?"

"Yes." He sighed. "End of story."

"Why won't you talk about it?"

"What was it he said... the energy created by our dreaming is like the air, it travels everywhere? Is that you want me to say to you, that we dreamed the same dream? Is that what you want to hear? Well, I'm not a wise shaman, a sun god made of gold, or a king who's been dead for five-hundred years. I'm a flesh and blood man who's fallible. I heard and saw enough on that mountain. I don't like other men fucking my woman, even if it *was* only in a dream."

"But those were *your* fantasies! It was *you* making love to me!"

"Lucid dreams, nightmares, fantasies, visions, what I need is a real, honest to God night's rest. After that last cat nap, I want shamans and kings and faceless strangers out of my bed and my head. What I need is you, Hope, always beside me, in my bed, every night, every morning."

"You're angry with Altahualpa."

"Yes! For his haunting you, for his haunting me, for his interfering with us! I'm an archaeologist, and you're an anthropologist on the threshold of a discovery that will make our names go down in history." He cupped the sides of his mouth and yelled across the cordillera, "But I have half a mind to let the Cave of Tears stay sealed for all eternity! Eternity... eternity... his voice echoed.

"Why?"

"Because *you* are the keeper of the half that makes *me* whole. You are *my* chosen one." He stabbed at his chest with his finger. "No obsession, no king's curse, will fuck with our refined energies, not as long as I draw a breath. All the treasures and riches and fame on earth can't measure up to what I feel for you in here." He patted his heart. "I'd like to take that stone sunburst hidden in your backpack and bust it up into smithereens."

"But you won't…"

"The king wasn't all bad, Hope. What he did to us was wrong, but his heart was in the right place. We do need to return what has been lost to the Temple of the Sun, you and I, humble servants of Viracocha, so that all the Children of the Sun may see the greatness that once ruled in Cuzco, the capital of the Inca empire, the navel of Pachamama. What is past *is* past, and it should no longer be hidden. The time to set things right is now."

"I think the king's heavy energies were weighing down his lighter ones. He was so brutally betrayed by Pizzaro. The Inca tradition demanded that after his death, Atahualpa be mummified and buried with all the treasure he had accumulated during his reign so the sun could call him back to another life on earth. Atahualpa was tricked into being baptized when he was waiting to be burned at the stake. He was promised he would be spared immolation and would instead enjoy the Christian death of strangulation. No sooner had he been garroted that Pizzaro reneged on his promise and burned the Inca's corpse."

Blake stopped walking and grabbed up her forearms so she was looking into his eyes. "When I said there wasn't an assistant willing to risk dysentery in a third world country for the chance to piece together the missing puzzles to a broken ceramic pot, when I said there wasn't a dedicated historian in the bunch, when I didn't believe you about not speaking Quechua, and your dreams, I was wrong, Hope." He gave her a shake. "If there is ever an assistant I'd want standing beside me, it's you. Know what's in my heart, sweet Hope-of-High-Hopes, know there will never again be any secrets between us because the truth is *waylluy*."

"I love you too, Blake. Maybe you partaking of The Vine of Life that one time opened the hard, stubborn place that closed when you were born." She tapped his head, and with a chuckle, he let her go. She unhooked her backpack, slid to her knees, fished inside it, and raised the stone sunburst up to him in an offering. "Take it, and let's get this show on the road. Lead me to where X marks the spot, and let's bring down that five-hundred-year-old wall barricading The Cave of Tears!"

"It's a good thing South American's are the most patient people I'll ever meet, *gringa*." His passion ignited and he dropped to his knees, tossing the stone disc aside. "But right now, I'm impatient for something else."

They worked on each other's clothing and finally got them off. His hands were everywhere, her hands were everywhere. Fierce, hot kisses reined down on every inch of skin. Raw restrained hunger surged to the surface as he positioned her on hands and knees. The round, fleshy curve of her ass was too enticing to resist, and he gave her a lusty smack that had her wiggling her cheeks in invitation for more.

"I love it that you're kinky," he said hoarsely, "but I'll save that for whenever you act like the brat you are." He bent over her, his chest hair brushing her back. His hands found her breasts and pulled at her nipples, tweaking them into even harder peaks. She began to shake all over as his hardness skimmed the crevice of her bottom, teasing her until she thought she would go mad. His hand found her vulva, parting her lips, slippery and soft and ready for him. His fingers delved in into her pussy with a deep, feverish rhythm, and she reached desperately back between her legs and caught his erection, guiding his cock, positioning him just where she wanted him. "I need you inside me," she begged. "Oh, God, please…"

Digging Up Destiny

He plunged into her, and her inner muscles clamped gratefully down around him. He fought to keep from coming; he wanted to enjoy this divine sensation for as long as possible; being buried inside her was heaven on earth. When he pulled free, a breeze chilled him, and it was better to be inside her hot, clutching core than to be outside. Her ass fitted perfectly into the curve of his groin as he drove into her harder and faster, banging his head against her cervix. He wondered if he was hurting her, but he needed to be that deep inside her. She allayed his fears by shoving her hips back, her flesh slapping against his flesh, meeting his every thrust, striving toward a lusty and swift culmination.

"Oh, I love what you're doing!" she gasped. When his hand cupped her mons, his thumb strumming the pinnacle of her pleasure, she surrendered to him in a burst of ecstasy that made her scream out his name, "Oh, Blake!"

His balls burned for her and contracted faster and faster, friction taking its toll on his control as the end of his cock exploded, shooting his cum deep into her womb.

Sagging forward, he held her close, and then they were lying on their sides pressed tightly together.

"What are you thinking?" she ventured, always curious.

"I'm thinking you're an amazing woman meant to be fucked often, and spanked ever so often!" He began laughing and she joined him. They only sobered up when earth began rumbling beneath them. Blake shielded her with his body. "Don't be scared, sweetheart, it happens all the time. It's just one of the many small earthquakes that erupt throughout the Andes."

Multicolored parrots squawked in fright and scattered from peaceful perches in a rain of wet leaves as animals crashed through the brush. Trees cracked and crashed to the ground somewhere in the distance. An eternity that only was mere minutes seemed to pass before the ground no longer shook, and then even the steady hum of jungle insects ceased in the eerie silence that followed.

He pushed to his feet, offering her his hand. Minds working in unison, they scrambled for their discarded clothing and dressed as quickly as they could. Sunburst tucked under one arm, he led her down the mountainside where the canopy grew even denser to the eyebrows of the jungle.

They emerged into a clearing riddled with ground holes resembling a blasted mine field. The Inca wall barricading the Cave of Tears and bearing the golden sunburst was gone – reduced to rubble mixed with a landside of earth that covered the entrance.

Blake tossed the stone disc into the brush like a Frisbee, rolled up his sleeves, picked up a shovel, speared it into the first pile, and began tossing dirt and rocks over his shoulder.

"Do you really believe the earthquake did this?" Hope broke the silence hours later, leaning her arms over the wooden handle of her shovel. She was drenched in sweat and bone- weary.

"You know as well as I do Atahualpa had to have the last laugh before he could finally rest in peace."

Side by side, long into the night, they continued doggedly digging up destiny, until the sun rose and Inti's rays illuminated their way into The Cave of Tears. Arm in arm, the Children of the Sun walked though the entrance enveloped in a circle of love and light.

Inside, Pachamama's dark womb gleamed with gold and silver.

Blake flicked on a flashlight, shining it into an endlessly dark tunnel.

Digging Up Destiny

"Munaway wiñaypaq!" a voice echoed deep within subterranean caverns followed by a short burst of mischievous laughter that quickly died away.

"Love me forever, my sweet Hope-of-High-Hopes," Blake whispered, answering her questing look.

THE END

Dreams & Desires

Laura Muir

Inspired by Alex Lifeson

Prologue

It all started normally enough – I was bored. On that day in my twenty-sixth year on earth, I seemed to reach the climax of boredom. So I decided I would go play beauty parlor, a luxury I rarely treated myself to on my part-time secretary's salary, but if I worked full-time and made more money, I'd never have the time or the energy – not to mention the inspiration – to write my poetry, and I like to think I have my priorities straight.

In the waiting room of the rather drab Dorchester, Massachusetts establishment, I flipped through the magazines scattered across the ugly coffee table. It was the usual assortment of *People* and *Cosmopolitan*, as appetizing as bonbons made of enriched white flour and pink sugar; absolutely no substance that would leave my profound self-esteem feeling sick afterwards. Then suddenly I spotted *Musician Magazine*. 'Oh good', I thought, as an attendant smilingly approached me and asked me if I was the one waiting to have my hair cut and dyed blonde. "Excuse me?" I blinked. When you have long, waving brown hair and someone asks you if you want to look factory produced, it is reason enough to want to kill yourself right there. "No," I replied, "brunettes are an endangered species; it would be an environmental crime." And I walked out, still holding *Musician Magazine*.

I took the train home, and the city looked unusually colorful behind the magic film of my tears, carefully concealed behind a pair of ultra-cool sunglasses. At least I was in Boston; that was my only consolation. Having adventured to Washington, Miami, London, Chicago and New York with the money I was supposed to have used for college, I could very well appreciate the quaint, toy-like ease of living in Dorchester, which I interpreted as Door-Chest-Her. Because the invisible door to my inner dimension was the only way out of the existential boredom that was slowly, but surely, suffocating my soul. Then I opened the magazine and saw him.

Chapter One

I got home and just sat gazing at the picture. There was a sunlit grave-yard behind him rising into the distance and crowned by a rainbow. He was sitting on an amp in front of a large window – through which this scene was visible – playing an electric guitar, his pose sublimely elegant; not at all contrived. I was fascinated; I had never seen such a strange ad. 'I thought everyone was afraid of graveyards', I thought. 'What a perverse marketing idea'. Then I noticed a little blonde boy running between the tombstones flying a red kite, and the soft, secret smile on the guitar player's lips told me it was him – his spirit free from the dull maturity that means giving up your dreams.

"Wow," I exclaimed out loud.

There was a hand-held telescope resting on the amp beside him, and this little detail made me feel happier than I had all day, all week, maybe even all month, but I've always been strange. 'We are literally the magic of starlight… that's the essence of a true, artistic vision… What a truly awesome ad'. And there was a delicate, colorful Japanese parasol lying at his feet. "He's gorgeous," I murmured. "Who the hell is he?"

"He's married." My roommate, Jackie, responded laconically.

I hadn't seen her passed out on the couch. "How do you know? You don't even know who I'm talking about."

"Any gorgeous man is already married, that's Murphy's law."

"Fuck Murphy."

"He can't get it up."

"It's no wonder."

* * *

fought all the mental demons one must deal with these days as I cut the page out of the magazine, throwing its useless bulk away, and pinned the picture on the side of my dresser so I could gaze at it as I lay in bed. But by the time I was ready to do so, I felt as emotionally ragged as if I had just crawled out of a cage in which I had been trapped with a mad dog; it's amazing how expertly our reason is trained to tear our feelings to pieces nowadays. 'What a pathetic little adolescent you are', my inner voice went right for my throat, 'mooning over a picture in a magazine just like a twelve-year-old. When will you ever grow up? When will you come down to earth? Life can be fun, just plain fun. Wait until you're old to be deep', and so on and so on. But then I got under the covers and curled up with the warm, feline mystery of my soul, all the daydreams inspired by gazing at him like insubstantial purrs exquisitely vibrating through my body.

'A man like him... I want a man like him', I chanted silently in my mind as I lit a candle and began drifting off feeling his small, shadowy form seated on my heart. 'Keep on playing, baby', I told him, 'don't let anyone stop you... play me to sleep... I'm so lonely... this life sucks... I love you, I don't care if you're married, you're still just a

sweet little boy... come into my dream-womb... I'll give you everything you want... I'll be your cosmic mistress... we'll meet in dreams
every night'...

I spotted him running between the gravestones with the colors of
the sunset streaming from his blood-red kite. I noticed with a sweet
thrill that I was nine-years-old again, and this made me very happy
because that had been my favorite age. I ran eagerly after him on the
opposite side of the field of tombstones, and met him at the other end.
He grinned at me and I smiled back shyly because he was a little older
than me and I already had a terrible crush on him.

"Who are you?" he asked.

"My name's Isabel," I said.

He laughed. "Is-a-bell. What a nice name!" he declared, so I dared
to ask him if I could fly his kite with him, which was still floating high
in the sky above him. "You have your own kite,' he told me.

"No I don't."

"Yes you do."

I noticed then the delicate silver string vanishing into the darkness
above my head.

"Come on!" He ran ahead of me, the tombstones shining cold as
ice under the full moon. I looked up and saw our kites crackling with
our laughter – his was blue-and-yellow, mine was red-and-yellow – and
as we ran we grew older; I could tell because the gravestones kept
shrinking until they were the size of ice cubes littering the grass like the
ruins of some wild party. He stopped with deliberate suddenness, forcing me to crash into his back, and it pleased me that he was mischievous. Turning around to face me, he laughed as he pulled the moon
down with his free hand and it shrank to the size of his fingertip. He

touched my lips with it, and I couldn't resist sucking on him tentatively at first, then more hungrily when he didn't protest.

"You're a bad girl," he whispered, and I surfaced swiftly but gently from the dream, my eyes opening to the sight of his image holding an electric guitar inside the halo of candlelight in the silent darkness of my bedroom, but my heart was throbbing as if it was my veins he was plucking, the images of my dream the song he had just played with me.

Chapter Two

The following night I dreamed with the Mansion for the first time. It was strange because I knew I was dreaming, and yet I felt as objectively alert as if I was awake. The minute I fell asleep I approached the gate. It looked frighteningly old and heavy emerging from the darkness with the dim glow of moon rock in a coiling, tangled pattern of living vines. This haunting gate was all I could see, but I knew there was a path beyond it leading into myself. I found myself imagining I had shrunk to an infinitely small size and was now inside my body, with the path behind the gate the artery leading to the mansion of my heart. And as I thought this, I saw the winding pattern of the gate as my own intestines, which was such a disconcerting experience that I quickly turned around and woke up.

For the rest of the night I couldn't sleep; there was an uncomfortable heaviness in my stomach that in the morning I concluded was the result of my cowardice. 'It would have been healthier to face what I was thinking no matter how strange it was', I thought. Yet I hypocritically listened to my rational voice, which was of the opposite opinion. I took the strange guitar ad down and all day treated myself like a dream-junkie, equating my feeling for Mystery with an addict's desire for hero-in, telling myself that dwelling on the dark wonder of my soul was not healthy; that just living life was what was important.

But lying in bed again that night, desperately missing him, my deepest self began to rebel again. 'Just live life', I thought sarcastically. 'Just skim the surface of everyday and have *fun*, that silly little bubble any thought too penetrating will instantly pop... deep feeling is the only truly enjoyable activity, so why the hell should I limit mine? That's just a clean, respectable form of suicide. How ironic that killing your body is a crime when we strangle our souls every day with cynical, so-called realistic thoughts. But my God, if we know anything by now it's that we don't know what reality is at all'. So I flung my bed sheet off with tri-umphant joy, as if it was a shroud, and by putting his picture back up I was rising above boredom and death; for me one and the same thing.

To my mingled pleasure and dismay, I found myself in front of the dream gate again. 'I have to go in. I can't be afraid of myself... I know I'm dreaming, so whatever's there is of my own making'. That was not as comforting a thought as I had hoped it would be, because, after all, how many undesirable influences had gone into making me? I was scared, but the gate began opening with a slow, reluctant reverence that reminded me of a wild animal backing away from a flaming torch. 'My spirit is the fire that is animating the substance of my body', I conclud-ed, like a first grader adding one plus one on the universal blackboard with a piece of chalk shaped like a crucifix. 'I want him to be there... if he's there then everything's good'...

I started down the path shining like a ray of moonlight, and remem-bered I had had this dream when I was a child, but that I had not been ready to pursue it then. I avoided looking at the black trees looming around me, their twisted limbs reflecting every negative thought I had ever had. I was wondering how deep into myself I would have to go before I ceased being surrounded by them and re-experiencing all my frustrated emotions like roots trying to grow against the concrete cynicism of the modern world. Then I saw it, a Mansion like the one in all the Gothic novels I had read as a child, with a window for every page I had turned – behind each one stretched the unknown space of a different plot furnished with ever-changing circumstances...

Only one window was lit at that moment, at the top right-hand corner of the house, moonlight glinting off the innumerable glass panes surrounding the sunlit warmth of the one inhabited room. I clearly remembered standing there as a dreaming child gazing up at it wondering who was in there, haunted by the formless force of the illumination because I could picture no one except myself, but that night I knew who it was. I *knew* him, I didn't know how, but I did, from ages ago, literally. We had met in some room – in some moment of time and space – inside the Mansion of history, which is really just the servants' quarters of the soul and the infinite wealth of dreaming... I saw him in a dark-blue velvet jacket offering me his hand, conscious of myself only as a low-cut violet dress and a tight corset pushing my breasts up to better enjoy the feel of his eyes on them... I laughed then in the dream because I knew my soul was like a child dressing up all the dolls of its incarnations with different styles of flesh and bone. 'How do I know all this'? I wondered. 'I don't, I'm just dreaming'... I became confused, and woke up.

Chapter Three

I was nervous about going to sleep for fear I would have silly, meaningless dreams instead of finding myself in front of the Mansion again, and sure enough, that's what happened. I woke up in the middle of the night sad and frustrated after a commercial-like stream of nonsensical images. I had fallen asleep in the dark, so I consoled myself by thinking that if I drifted off staring at the candle flame illuminating his image, and thinking the fixed thought of dreaming with him again, that I could make it happen. After all, when we get in a car or on a plane we have a destination in mind; we know where we're going. So why should we fall asleep like lazy hitchhikers to get picked up by any obnoxious dream that happens to come along? Needless to say, the modern psyche is a crowded place full of conceptual traffic jams; who knows what to believe these days. All I knew was that the power of my desire was a fuel I didn't want to waste. I had found a dream in this man, and my heart decided to go for it rather than remaining doubtfully parked in my mind because the magical road is invisible, and there are very few fueling stations provided by other similarly adventurous and spirited souls along the way.

I decided to follow a disciplined ritual, prepared to gradually stretch my super-sensual muscles, realizing that training my awareness to handle the freedom of dreams was probably going to be as hard as becoming physically limber enough to express my feelings by dancing. I can't literally execute the movements I see in my head when listening to music, and in the same way I can conceive of another more fluid dimension – of a dream space where I can meet him. 'But if I want to do that, I have to work at it; I have to get off the rational wheelchair of only believing in the limitations of mortality and start flying inside without fear of falling into a meaningless grave in the end'.

I bought a box of expensive violet candles, because I didn't want any cheap wax dripping all over the place like doubtful thoughts cluttering the serenity of my willpower, and because violet has the highest frequency vibration of all colors; it is the last shade on the visible spectrum, which made the long, slender line of the candle an appropriate symbol of the division between my waking consciousness and my dream awareness. I lay staring at the gently flickering flame thinking that my body was the red end of the spectrum – the dense matter which the ultra-violet energy of my spirit temporarily inhabits. And the invisible part of the spectrum corresponds to my dream body, which feels much more intensely than my waking self even though it seems insubstantial. While I'm awake, I'm on the visible side of the spectrum, while I'm asleep I'm on the side invisible to my physical eyes, and my soul is both of these at once, somehow… and maybe what life is all about is growing into the full range of my being…

I was in front of the Mansion again and his window was still lit.

"All right!" I cried, but then felt like a silly cheerleader applauding some astronomical athletic feat and thought it best to behave a little more maturely. I had managed to return to the same dream three times, which was encouraging, but the mysterious game had only just begun. I was up against impossibility in all its unshakable strength, yet since he appeared to be the prize, I was more than willing to brave it. 'Okay, first things first... I have to walk through the front door... or do I have to create one first so I can walk through it? But if there isn't a door, then I can just walk in... but if there isn't one, what will I be walking in through'? I was becoming confused watching all these thoughts float past my mind's eye as if I was standing at the bottom of the ocean – at the base of all manifestation. 'If I keep on being so literal I'm going to drown from the weight of all the possibilities surrounding me. I have to become a mermaid and just flow with my imagination... but not literally', I added quickly, afraid I would develop a tail and fins, and not having legs to spread for him would transform the dream into a nightmare.

Then suddenly I was standing in a dim corridor, and it was such a pleasantly effortless change that I curiously studied the wallpaper – miniature couples in Victorian dress walking a small dog. They were all over the faded yellow wall dressed in brown, and I began to feel terribly oppressed. I had to get out of there; this was not the way to him at all. 'I'm inside my conditioning', I thought, and didn't question my diagnosis because it came from a part of me that sounded very calm and sure of itself. My emotions latched onto this part of me like children clinging to their parent, trusting my own higher awareness to get me the hell out of there. But nothing happened, so I considered the desperate measure of waking up, yet I didn't know how to go about it without the moonlit gate as a reference. I felt I had gone too deep to surface so quickly, and I knew I had to pass through this oppressive corridor if I was ever going to be the mistress of my dreams and enjoy the pleasure of meeting him there.

I started walking in the direction I was facing, and almost immediately there was a door on my left. I didn't think; I just opened it gratefully, and found myself in what struck me as a waiting room because of the neat row of chairs lined up against one wall and the coffee table littered with magazines. That was where all resemblance to earthly waiting rooms ended, however, for the chairs were each little universes – deep black cloth glittering with stars – and the soft, plush carpet was the light-green of a sunlit Caribbean sea. The colorful magazines ware arranged on the crystal table in the shape of a rainbow, and I curiously studied their titles: *Creative Biology; Galactic Cultures; The Art of Sense; 3D Painting; Dimensions Through Music; Virtual to Real*. I laughed in delight.

"Can I help you?"

I wheeled around, but there was no one else in the room with me, the violet walls shining and grooved like a seashell. 'Who's there?" I asked politely, even though she was rudely intruding on my dream.

"You are." It sounded like my own voice.

"Oh… I suppose there's a moral in this, that the only person who can help me is myself, or something to that effect."

"Is a moral what you want?"

"No, I want him."

"No matter what?"

"Now that's a good question, because in dreams there's no such thing as matter, right?"

"Right."

"Then yes, I want him, no matter what."

"And what will you do when you get him?"

"Well... I'm not going to *get* him, I mean, I'll never have him in the sense of owning him, I just want to meet him... and dream with him..."

I found myself in another room abruptly. 'I guess I'm going to have to get used to these instant changes. But what if I like where I am and don't want it to go away? I've got to figure out how to hold onto it'.

I looked around me. I was in a bedroom. That was obvious because there was a bed behind me. Then I panicked, because he was lying on it. I looked away. 'Okay, this is getting serious'... I tried to calmly and objectively study my surroundings, the room having become a haze of colors and forms at the explosively unexpected sight of him; my control shattered. 'Oh, Jesus, I don't even know him... but this is only a dream... I feel like a spider... did I catch him in the web of my dreaming? Am I seeing him as he looks lying on his own bed now? I should let him go... no, wait, there's no hurry, he seems to be sleeping peacefully; I'm not disturbing him by embracing him with my imagination'... I glanced back at him for a split second, as if he was the sun illuminating my own dream around me and if I looked directly at him I would go blind to impossibility and see only the vision of my heart.

I focused on the dark wooden dresser topped by an oval mirror framed by purple cloth. Since there was no time in sleep there was no need to rush things, yet at the same time I was worried it would soon be morning. But as I stared at the soothing velvet, I knew that time here was like its thick, soft folds... an uninterrupted flow of feeling undulating with currents, each shadowy fold the depth of a night... the dark arch of heaven over the world of a dream... I had only to touch it with my heart by remembering it and the egg of the mirror would crack into a bolt of lightning as it came to life around me.

There was no need for me to worry about permanence and all the forms it takes in the real world because they're only the wood that shoots off the sparks of possibilities filling my personal eternity like stars in the night sky... the sensual friction of infinite imaginations coming into contact with each other...

Finally, I was ready to face him lying on the bed. I turned and stared at him. The room was beautifully rich, as was befitting his presence in it, drapes of glowing colors hanging everywhere like the rainbow of all my lonely tears evaporated around his golden-haired warmth. He was curled up beneath the sea-green sheet beneath the deep weight of sleep surrounded by the currents of dreams, his lips curving up softly from the pull of one. 'He's pleased he's here', I thought, approaching him slowly, and only just then noticing that the floor was made of sand, the fine white sand found on Caribbean beaches, and that I was wearing a very strange swimsuit made of wet seaweed clinging to me with disturbing tenacity, as though it was alive; it wrapped around my body and between my thighs as if I had drowned.

'This must symbolize all the physical laws I'm defying to meet him here in the high-class hotel of dreaming... no cheap neon sign for us, this one glows the molten red of volcanoes and glitters sea-foam and starlight'...

I very gently knelt on the edge of the bed and gazed down at him. I wanted to wake him, but I was worried he might disappear if I did. I had to be very gentle about it so as not to rouse him completely, only in the dream. 'Oh, God, he's so handsome'. His bare arm and neck were almost too real for me to handle the sight of; they were a deliciously heavy weight in the delicate grasp of my dreaming awareness. I looked at the different parts of him, building a nest for my soul with him as I lifted the sheet off him slowly, holding my breath as its cresting wave threatened to drown me with the full experience of his naked body.

"I'm terrible," I whispered, and he opened his eyes. I froze, torn between the penetrating power of his stare and the warm flesh of his bare thighs and the beautiful cock that was wide awake between them.

"What the hell?" he murmured sleepily, rolling onto his back. 'Where am I?"

"You're just dreaming."

"Oh…" He smiled. "In that case…" He pulled me down on top of him.

I lost myself as my hands explored the reassuringly firm world of his chest, and our tongues rolled around and around together like naked bodies in the warm cave of our joined mouths, open to a primeval ocean… our two beings were energetic fish leaping joyfully around each other… two dolphins rising from the depths of the darkness and diving back in, all possible experiences contained beneath their joyous arches breaking in sprays of starlight…

I surfaced with a huge effort of will, raising my awareness up out of the delicious, drowning weight of his arms as I sat up. I didn't want to lose myself, and the sensual reality of him as a naked man, by turning into a dolphin or something ridiculous like that.

"Wow." He grinned. "Kissing is fun when you're asleep… although I've done it before and it was never like this, you're a very special dream. And if kissing you is such a trip…" He was going to pull me down on top of him again, but I slipped out of his grasp and crawled to the foot of the bed, gazing at him from a safer distance. He sat up, looking around him. "What a great room… it's like being on stage under all the lights… I get it, you're my guitar. Come here and let me tune you up."

I just stared at him, desperately wondering how I could submit to him while still holding my imagination under control and keep us there.

"Come on, sweetheart," he reached for me, "let's play."

"No, wait!" I pleaded, having concluded that if this was ever going to work he had to be in on it; he couldn't just go off and leave me holding the wild manes of both our imaginations like two spirited horses unsaddled by any limitations.

He grabbed me. "Don't expect me to sweet-talk you when you're not even real."

"I am so!" I pulled away from him again. "You happen to be in *my* dream, you know."

"Okay, I'm sorry." He smiled indulgently. "I'll be nice to you even though you don't exist."

I slapped him, to my amazement, but obviously he was insulting me.

"Jesus!" he whispered. "That should have woken me up..." He pushed me back across the bed and pinned my arms over my head, thrusting his knee between my legs and arching his body over mine. "That felt very real," he said quietly, and my swimsuit disintegrated like ancient mummy wrappings blown away by the timeless wind of his breath as he caressed my arms slowly from the wrists down to my delicate breasts. "And if that felt real, so will this..."

"Before you do anything you might regret," I forced myself to say even as I raised my legs willingly around him, "I have to warn you that this is not an ordinary dream you're having..."

"I already know that." He kissed my lips while teasing the hot heart of my pussy with the cool head of his erection.

My labial lips eagerly kissed his thick firmness, which felt very much like a dream come true. "Oh, God, promise you'll meet me here again tomorrow night," I begged.

He laughed. "Sure, I promise."

"No, I mean it. When you go to sleep, will you think about coming back here?"

"That all depends on how good you feel…"

The shock of his thrust was so deep and sweet that I forgot it wasn't real and suddenly woke up alone in my bedroom, the glorious weight of his strong body replaced by a crushing loneliness against my heart.

Chapter Four

rolled over into his arms and we opened our eyes at the same time. He smiled as if pleased to see me again, but then I saw a frown crease his brow and I knew he was considering all the negative psychological interpretations of a recurring dream. I sensed part of him was a little worried about returning to a fantasy when his life was already so fulfilling, but the creativity of his feelings was a natural thing to him as a musician, so after a moment the black flock of mental doubts went away and he smiled another pure ray of sunshine at me. I sighed, and cuddled comfortably in his arms.

"That wasn't very fun, waking up at the moment of truth last night," he said, holding me close.

"You have to help me,' I told him. 'This isn't a normal dream… I saw the ad you did for *Musician Magazine*."

His eyes narrowed as he pulled away slightly and stared down at my face. "That was you in that other dream, too, wasn't it?"

"The one where we were running through the graveyard flying comet kites and you told me I was a bad girl?"

"Yes!"

"Help me," I gasped between kisses. "Please remember that we're dreaming and that anything we can imagine we'll experience..." My awareness alone struggling to brace the dream around us without his help was like a bird with only one wing soaring in the heaven of our combined pleasure. I needed him to consciously believe in the unlimited possibilities open to us; to realize that our shared ecstasy was literally the charged atmosphere of worlds exploding out of his thrusts inside the living space of my womb. I tried to tell him this between kisses, like a metaphysical school teacher instructing a deeply spoiled but highly promising student. Then I felt the smooth glide of his erection down my pussy's slick runway and we ascended together... his violent surge of action between my thighs was devastating... I began seeing volcanoes erupting and tidal waves crashing...

"What the hell?" He raised his head and looked down into my eyes. "I was just inside a *National Geographic* special!"

"I told you, I need your help!"

"What should I do?"

"Use your imagination like you would your hands..."

He braced himself on one arm and caressed me slowly with his left hand, dwelling on my small but shapely breasts, twirling his thumb around and around one of my dark-rose aureoles and bringing my long nipple to almost painful attention. He slid his glorious hard-on slowly in and out of my gratefully tight pussy, which had been empty of a man for much too long. "An island," he murmured, pulling out of me abruptly and studying the curves of my slender body resting against the sea-green sheet... his blue eyes becoming my sky, his blonde hair rays of light flowing around me as he reached down to kiss me... I was inhaling him, his breath was a warm tropical breeze, and my mind was relaxed and lazy as a palm leaf absorbing the timeless beauty of our mysteriously divine natures... he thrust his cock back inside me, plunging his full length into my begging wet depths over and over again, as salty tears stung my eyes from the waves of pure joy breaking between my thighs. "This is more like it..." I heard the breeze of his whisper and saw a pleasure ship cruising across water stained by a vivid sunset to the color of blood... I was standing at a great height, leaning against the black skeleton of a window looking down at a lush green island where a couch was camouflaged amidst huge banana leaves strewn with strawberry cushions... "Oh, yes!" he breathed, and our growing ecstasy kept dimensions fluid... I was reclining on the couch watching him play his guitar as a jeweled butterfly hovered around him its wings catching the sunlight beating in rhythm to his notes flowing on the current of the melody. There was a freshly sewn field spread open behind him, and I felt each furrow as the path between my legs he was passionately plowing to nourish the sense of himself, reaping the harvest of his pleasure over and over again...

I opened my eyes and the halo of candlelight was the frail ghost of the dream sun into which we had both dissolved in a burning climax. The pleasure had been so real I couldn't be sad that I hadn't woken up in his arms; I felt so fulfilled it didn't really matter. I was happy to know he was free to intersect with me in a dream whenever he pleased, and I was filled with confidence he would want to again.

I sighed, curling up comfortably on my bed. I could almost feel him lying on his own mattress countless miles away, perhaps holding his wife in his arms and thinking it was her he had been caressing as he slept, and that might even be the case, but I wasn't jealous. It was *my* imagination he had entered, *my* soul he had caressed with his, and I knew when he went to bed tomorrow night that he would think of me and that we would meet again behind the closed shades of our eyelids in the room of our minds, the atmosphere of our hearts sustaining the body of whatever world we desired to shape around us.

Chapter Five

"I have tickets to a concert tonight, you wanna go?" Jackie confronted me in the hallway that morning as we were both getting ready for work.

"No thanks, I've got a dream to catch." I walked into the bathroom and started putting on my make-up.

"Uh-huh, you sure do." She leaned in the doorway with her arms crossed complacently beneath her breasts, eyeing me like a cat who finally has the maddeningly elusive bird of my heart safely trapped. "The man in that ad you're so fucking crazy about is the guitarist of this band, and I happen to have twelfth row seats."

I stared at her, the world crashing down around me. The corners of sidewalks and rooms and the hands of clocks were blocks of rubble tragically separating me from him; the delicate imaginative thread connecting me directly to him in dreams disappearing amidst the solid complexity of reality.

"And I might even be able to swing backstage passes," she added lightly. "But, since you don't want to go..." She turned away.

"No!" I screamed. "Yes!"

So, he had been dreaming with me while he was on the road, checking into the luxurious pleasures of my psyche as his body lay in his hotel room. I had been able to handle the reality of his wife, but the idea of groupies made me sick.

* * *

"They don't take groupies," Jackie reassured me in the car on the way to the concert that night. "They're famous for being weird like that. They're the hottest band around, but they don't even party. They like to go back to the hotel and have ice cream and crash out, if you can believe it. I'm glad I got these passes so you can meet him. You'll get him out of your system when you realize he's really just a normal, married man going on forty."

Being familiar with some of the dreams he had, I knew "crashing out" for him was a thousand times more exciting than any earthly party could be. "Why are you going to see them if you're so cynical about them?" I asked.

"Because they're a hot band." Jackie brought the conversation to a fulfilling end.

I was merely one of the hundreds of ant-size fans filing into the vast concert hall. For me the space of this night felt like an egg the intense warmth of his music and his presence together would crack open into another dimension altogether. The concert hall looked like a huge nest to me, the twigs of countless wooden seats rising around me, and my imagination was the precious living egg the band's music was going to incubate with the mysterious warmth of manifested soul and help bring to life around me, somehow...

I tolerated the roaring noise of the opening band like a prisoner before a firing squad knowing the ecstasy of heaven is next, my per-spiring palm holding onto my backstage pass with a sweet terror, as if it was a ticket into the next world and the presence of angels. Then at last there was a pregnant darkness and in a rainbow flood of lights the real show began.

Maybe I was biased, but I thought the drums were too loud and that the guitar wasn't turned up enough, yet it seemed befitting to the concert ritual – the united pounding of thousands of hearts, the strumming and plucking of individual feelings and thoughts taking the back seat. Except during the guitar solos, when everyone's desires seemed to scream out at once in the drawn out electrical notes, his fingertips flying across the strings making me think of all the tiny particles physicists say compose matter, and everything was real for me because of him, *for* him.

The lightshow, complete with lasers, was spectacular, especially during the drum solo. A rainbow of colors shone off the white-and-silver set so it looked like a cosmic flower, its petals a pure bloom revolving like a galaxy in the darkness. It was stunning, as was watching my dream man gliding around on the current of the music like an immortal boy playing in the waves of feeling flowing towards him from the dark, living ocean of the audience beyond the shore's luminous stage. He wandered over to his effects board a few times, and I was upset for him, thinking that if he was in one of my dreams he wouldn't have any technical problems; the laws of manifestation would obey him smoothly, perfectly.

Then two minutes later the show was over. It had actually lasted over two hours, but I couldn't believe it when he raised his guitar, smiled, and ran off the stage, his body in a loose, dark-blue cotton suit slender yet exquisitely full. They came back for an encore, and it was the highlight of the night when he performed an orgasmically long solo, rays of violet light shining over his head smoking into a cloud as if from the sensual intensity of the melody, his playing hands caressing the invisibly vibrating flesh of the guitar and of my soul.

Then they were gone for good and terror struck me like a blast of arctic air. There was no way in hell I was going backstage. "Jackie... um..."

"Let's go!"

"Um... no..."

"What? Are you kidding? I killed myself to get these passes for you!"

"Okay, but I want you to know that I'm absolutely terrified, and that there's no point in it. They're just going to look at us for a second and then blink over to the next person. We'll be brushed away by their lashes like particles of dust..." I ranted as she led the way backstage.

It was awful being one of the anonymous nobodies seeking entrance into the Presence, slinking like cats past the frightening watchdogs of the roadies when, after all, he was already happily neutered to any possible romantic adventure by years of marriage. Besides, a sordid little interlude was hardly what I had in mind. So why was I going backstage, to see if he would recognize me? Well, what if he did? It wouldn't change anything. I could still be with him only in dreams. Yet it would be proof of magic if he knew me, and I could hold this proof for the rest of my life like a genie bottle from which my feelings could caress dreams without end. That was the sublime theory with which I armored myself as we entered the room where the band was resting. I knew it was a bunch of bullshit, however, because what I wanted was *him*, in the flesh, its experience dream enough for a lifetime. Nevertheless, I donned the halo of my spiritual vision of him, hiding behind Jackie like an angel purely unfamiliar with earthly introductions. Then I saw she had brought a CD with her to be autographed and I panicked, thinking I would simply hold out my hand for his signature, its scrawl a cosmic wavelength of power and pleasure everyone was dying to live on but could only do so vicariously through him.

She stepped aside and Alex looked at me with a smiling "I'll do you next" expression, a subliminal boredom making his features sag a little so he looked a little older than in my dreams. 'He doesn't recognize me', I thought with the cold finality of an executioner's blade falling over the vulnerable neck of my imagination. All that was left was the empty body of my circumstances. Fortunately, however, the fact that I was in pieces was not literally visible, so I pulled myself temporarily together and turned to go.

Someone gently but firmly grasped my arm. "I'm leaving!" I hissed, thinking it was Jackie trying to stop me.

'Wait just a minute, please," I heard him say, and turned around again. He stared at my face, and suddenly there was no one else in the room; the crowd and the noise filtered away like in a movie when the camera focuses on something close-up and everything else becomes an insignificant blur. "At the risk of sounding trite, don't I know you?" he asked, smiling, but his eyes were sober.

"We flew comets together one night," I replied, and instantly saw the memory of them shining beautifully in his blue irises. "I think I can also tell you what you dreamed last night, and the night before that."

He glanced around him, and I saw again the people standing by as anonymous as wax figures waiting to be lit up by his attention. "Let's get out of here." He took my arm again and I glanced back at Jackie to experience the pleasure of watching her staring after me in absolute shock.

Chapter Six

He took me into a dressing room, and the joy of what was happening made me feel like a bird flying in through a window – the small space could scarcely contain my excitement as my heart beat like wild wings crashing against the sight of my incredulously smiling image in a mirror. I looked beautifully elegant in my form-fitting pearl-gray coat, a striking contrast to my intensely dark eyes. I turned to face him.

"Won't you sit down?" He offered me a chair with a gracious smoothness that made me fall even more painfully in love with him. He seated himself across from me, and I fingered my black leather gloves nervously. "This is an interesting situation, to say the least," he commented, and I nodded, more helplessly limp than my gloves, needing his interest, his love, to come alive; I felt that if he wasn't going to be a part of my life that I might as well just hang it all up. I stared down at my lap.

"Look at me." It was a gentle command. "You *are* her…" His voice was soft, as if he was talking to himself.

"I'm sorry," I said.

"Why?"

"Because… I feel like an intruder who broke into your life through the back dream door."

He smiled. "It's okay. You're more than welcome… Isabel?"

I smiled because he had remembered my name.

"Wow, this is strange…" He looked away and I could see he was feeling a little confused, the faint wrinkles next to his mouth and eyes revealing his age. They were almost invisible when he was smiling, but now they became painfully apparent, like lines across the paper of his flesh on which were clearly written for me his thoughts – his wife, his children and his devotion to his music formed the equation of his life, but now there was me, a stray figure with no place in it, except that I was included in the sum of his fulfillment.

"I'm sorry," I repeated, then thought it best to be a little more articulate and began telling him how I had felt when I saw the picture of him in *Musician Magazine*. I described the Manor to him, and explained how, encouraged by the idea of meeting him in dreams, I had begun to follow a disciplined ritual in which the main ingredient was really believing magic was possible, and remembering the magazines in the cosmic waiting room, I told him their titles because I thought he would like them. "And I guess you know the rest." I wrapped up my little speech with the classic ribbon of this phrase, and handed it over to him. For me it was a glorious gift, but I was afraid he was looking at me with mistrust, as if there was a bomb concealed inside the luminous packaging, which made me wonder if exploding the limits of possibility was a good thing.

"This is strange…" he repeated, and I was overjoyed because it meant he wasn't going to dismiss the whole thing away by calling it a coincidence. I wished I knew what more to say, but the only thing that came to my mind was "I love you" and that hardly seemed appropriate at the moment. It would have been like handing him a heavy, heart-shaped stone as he floated above the earth in the unconditional space our dreaming together had opened up around us: he would either crash to earth with the sudden weight of my feeling for him, my life abruptly in his hands, or he would drop me flat. So I kept quiet. I had to make my open silence a parachute for him so he could bring the freedom of heaven down to solid reality slowly, with enough time to emotionally integrate them. "I'm glad you came tonight," he said finally. "Now at least I know I wasn't making you up."

My heart stopped. In a second he was going to get up and go back to signing CD's, dismissing the fact that we had made love in another dimension, not a common occurrence, to say the least, but definitely strange enough to make forgetting it a politely acceptable solution. I stood up. Being with him in dreams when he had nothing else to do was one thing, but now I was selfishly taking time off his life. "I won't keep you," I murmured.

He grasped one of my hands. "You don't have to go yet, do you?"

I sat down again, almost literally collapsing into the chair with joy. "Oh, no," I said, "I just thought you had to get back…"

"No, I don't…" One moment he was leaning towards me in a small room, and the next his mouth was the whole world; all the adventure and excitement I could ever want offered to me in the seriously playful adversary of his tongue.

Chapter Seven

"What happened? What the hell happened?!" Jackie was a little hysterical.

"Nothing."

"Nothing? I'm going to kill you, Isabel! Out with it."

"Not now, I have to go to sleep."

"Go to sleep?!"

I paused in the midst of my before bed preparations to stare at her a moment, hoping my calm gaze would soothe her apoplectic condition.

"You just walk away with him," she gasped, "as if you've known each other forever, and you say nothing happened! Okay, we're going to sit down now and you're going to tell me everything." She grasped my shoulders and pushed me down onto the couch like an adult taking a willful child in hand determined to find out the full extent of his mischievousness. I was miserable, and this treatment made me feel even more foolishly young and vulnerable. I burst out crying, tears coming much easier than words and expressing much more. "Oh, my God, what happened?!" she wailed sympathetically.

"I love him!" I sobbed. "I love him!"

"Oh, my God." She fell back across the couch, fatally run through with curiosity. "Oh, please, have mercy, please, tell me what happened," she moaned.

"There's nothing to tell... I love him, but he's married and has children and he's very busy, so we can only be together in dreams." I folded my hands in my lap and sat perfectly still as if posing for my portrait framed by these tragic facts.

She sat up slowly, reminding me of a vampire rising in her coffin, and stared at me with a voracious anger. I had bled her dry with suspense yet offered only the lifeless afterworld of dreams in return. Her short, dyed red hair blazed like a fire through the film of my tears.

"We kissed," I sighed, regretfully offering her this precious morsel of fact.

"You kissed," she echoed matter-of-factly. "You kissed." Her cold, sharp voice made the statement feel like a bullet piercing my heart. "I suppose he saw you and thought you were so irresistible that he whisked you off somewhere and attacked you. Love at first sight, you know, like in the movies. Is that all? Why didn't you say so, it happens all the time; it's no big deal."

"If you don't shut-up, Jackie, I'm going to shove the fire poker up your cold little cunt."

"What...?" I sensed she was filled with sudden respect for me, because I had never said anything so wonderfully down-to-earth.

"Okay, I'll give it to you straight, even though you won't believe it." And I explained to her how we had met in dreams, that he had recognized me, and we had gone into a dressing room to ponder the highly unusual situation where we kissed for a while, but then we concluded it was wrong and that the best thing would be to continue dreaming together and enjoy exploring that dimension, which couldn't hurt anyone. "And we're going to write each other to keep in touch, and so we know we really are having the same dreams."

"Now why wouldn't I believe that?" she asked calmly, falling back across the couch again. "Really, Isabel, you should have just said so..." She sat up again abruptly, like a wire springing back to her normal rigid range of perception. "Are you trying to drive me insane?!"

I shook my head. "No, and that's why I want to go to sleep, because we agreed to meet again tonight, but then only every other night after this, to absorb whatever experiences we might have and give us a little time to write each other about it."

She fell hack across the couch a third time, and I thought of those stick birds they used to sell in liquor stores that go hack and forth into the glass and out of it – poor Jackie dipping the stiff beak of her cynical reason into the intoxicatingly enchanting brew of my story. "You aren't kidding, are you?" she said in a choked voice. "And I have to believe you because I saw the way he looked at you..."

"Oh, please, tell me about it!" I wanted to re-live the joy of his recognition; I wanted her to describe his expression when I was too busy panicking to notice it.

"Well, he looked at you and you turned around right away. I felt like strangling you for being such a fucking coward, but then I noticed he had a funny look on his face..."

"Describe it!"

"He looked surprised, and he stopped smiling... now that I think about it, he did look a little stunned... when he grabbed your arm, I thought he was just being nice and telling you not to be shy, but apparently there was a lot more than that going down!"

"I'll say... I have to go! Good night." I shot up off the couch and ran into my bedroom as if an alarm had gone off. I had to get to bed. I had to go to sleep. He was waiting for me. I locked my door against Jackie and stripped quickly, lighting my last violet candle in the darkness. 'I have to buy more tomorrow'. It was a glorious thought, because they were my magical road to him. I would burn enough of them to reach all the way to wherever he really lived so that maybe one day we could really be together...

Drops of water had glistened like stars on the window pane behind him. I saw them each time I surfaced from a kiss feeling as if I was reenacting the moment when life first emerged from the ocean as I separated myself from his deliciously fluid companionship, only to become aware of the exciting pleasure of merging with him again. We had escaped the arena through a back door and he had accompanied me home in a cab. I had convinced myself the ride would never end; that as he kissed me we would slip into a dream and the brief space of the night around us would become an endless darkness in which each little trembling light was the sun of worlds we could enter and live whenever we pleased...

He drew back slightly, unbuttoning my coat halfway so he could slip his hands into it and caress my breasts through my shirt as we kept kissing.

"Damn," he whispered, angry at all the dead cloth separating us.

I couldn't resist what I did next; I looked up into his eyes and unzipped his pants before he could protest.

He gazed back at me in wonder, and I suddenly realized this hadn't really happened. We were both sleeping and had returned to the cab in our dream. He smiled, encouraging me to go on, and I was very pleased to notice there was no driver to observe us; the car was moving on its own through the darkness, and the city lights were now really stars as I had imagined them to be.

"See, this isn't so bad," he told me quietly, caressing my long dark hair, and I moaned when I felt how real his cock was, warm, soft, full. Mysteriously, his penis contained all of him, and he was in my mouth; his feelings were all concentrated inside me. I washed my tongue over his stiffening length and a wave of light flowed across the windshield in the corner of my eye. As his pleasure intensified, the car began vibrating as if it was traveling at too high a speed. I looked up at him, a little concerned, but his eyes ware closed so I kept sucking him down fervently, using all the skills I had learned and ones I didn't even know I possessed. His amazingly hard dick inspired me as no other erection ever had into literally worshipping it with my sensually dancing tongue twirling around and around him like Salome wrapping him in her seven warm and misty veils; the firm ring of my lips sliding up and down his demanding length wedding the deepest most primal parts of me to blessed service of his pleasure which was hauntingly indistinguishable from mine as I willingly cut off my breath by burying his head in my neck as far as I dared, encouraging him to shove it in deeper still by placing his hands on my head and moaning for him to use it as he willed. When he climaxed, a luminous tidal wave crashed against the windowpane, its pure white foam illuminating the darkness all around us as the cab slowly came to a stop. Everything was perfectly still as I licked my lips, still starving with desire for him, but content for the moment. He smiled at me, holding my dark eyes with his gently lucid yet intensely playful blue ones, brushing my hair away from my mouth where it had tangled into a sticky web around him.

"I wonder where we are," he whispered in the profoundly peaceful silence. He looked out the window behind me and I looked out the one behind him.

We were on a white beach at the birth of the dawn, that precious moment when the sun's rays first emerge like fingers lovingly caressing the horizon.

"Let's get out," I suggested, just as he had the same idea and opened his door. He pulled me out of the cab quickly, and I wondered at his sudden urgency until I saw what I had thought of as a car fall apart and become the two halves of a giant oyster shell.

"Come on," he said, "let's explore."

Chapter Eight

think Jackie decided that since she couldn't understand what had happened between Alex and me that nothing really had. I think she regressed to her first impression – that he had grabbed my arm to tell me not to be shy. I don't really know how she filed the whole thing away in her mind, but the result was that we said even less to each other than normal. But this wasn't important; my dreams with Alex were all that mattered.

It was strange, though, how I could do anything with him in dreams without being embarrassed, yet I couldn't put a single word down on paper when I tried to write him what I was feeling. 'He doesn't care about me except when he's sleeping, and that's not very flattering', I kept thinking.

DearAlex was as far as I got trying to write him that first week, but as a result of always holding a pen in my hand like a director's baton poised over the orchestra of my love for him, I began scribbling verses. I didn't take them seriously at first; they were just entertaining crumbs I threw the fat, lazy pigeon hours at the office waiting for my bi-nightly flight to an erotic paradise. But suddenly two lines fell together, then four, then six

Dreams & Desires

like the cars of a train linking so I could ride my feelings for him and in turn offer him its adventure. The first poem I wrote for him was like a song – short verses that rhymed – and I found myself reciting them in the midst of my daily activities, a sense of life's unconditional magic always with me now, even when I was filing thigh-high piles of invoices.

Time passes eternally along your smile
The dimples of past and future
As endless dreams like purrs arise
From your soul's warmth caressed by mine

I'll never be with you
It isn't possible
But I'm not realistic·
Magic isn't logical

I must face that you are taken
From selfish dreams awaken
Settle for the men I meet
To circumstances admit defeat
But if I was your little girl
Would you tell me tales of magic worlds?

I'll never be with you
It isn't possible
But I'm not realistic
Magic isn't logical

I was singing the chorus one day as I fixed myself some dinner and Jackie heard me. She suddenly appeared in the kitchen doorway, and I grinned at her. This seems to have been a mistake, because she exploded.

"I can't take it!" she yelled. "You're driving me insane! What's going on? What *is* this?" She shook something at me, and since my awareness was a little shell-shocked from her screaming, it took me a second to realize it wasn't the white flag of her emotional breakdown and surrender she was offering me but an envelope. "It's a letter for you from him! What the hell's going on, Isabel? And don't give me any shit about dreams. Are you blackmailing him? Are you pregnant? Tell me the truth or I won't give it to you."

I didn't fling the kitchen knife at her only because I was afraid of staining his precious envelope. "Calm down, Jackie, just give it to me and we'll read it together, how's that?"

She stared at me a moment, but then handed the letter to me and stood looking over my shoulder. It was a curse, to say the least, to have to share this moment with her, and I was so terrified he was writing to tell me we couldn't dream together anymore that I just stared blindly at his cursive as if it was the EKG of my heartbeat in its final moments.

"These are some of the dreams I've had with you," Jackie read out loud. *"Let me know if they're true."* Oh, my God, you weren't kidding... I don't believe this!"

I started walking away, taking advantage of her immobile shock.

"Hey, wait a minute..."

I ran.

"Isabel, you bitch!"

I slammed my bedroom door and locked it, diving onto my bed and his descriptions of our dreams.

They were brief outlines of what we had experienced, and I smiled at the way he got around describing what had happened when we returned to the cab, and other similar occurrences, by writing, *And then you were a bad girl again.* But despite the skeletal brevity of his account and its corresponding lack of emotion, I could still feel the warmth of his reaction the way I had in the dream. The aura of his spirit illuminated my room like light burning through the thin cloth of a lampshade, the walls and objects aglow with his pleasure, their dimensions the hinges of sleep's dark door where the energetic limbs of our imaginations entwined and worlds were fashioned by the waves of our pleasure. I knew this was so without having to build any huge complex machines to test my ideas the way modern physicists do. I understood particles and waves in other terms – as his organs and emotions, his muscles and his feelings, as his thoughts and his touch, his being the eternal reality of which they were the experiential parts.

He signed *Alex* with no term of endearment, but at least with no coolly removed *Sincerely* or *Affectionately*. Just *Alex*, which was more than enough for me.

"Isabel..." Jackie knocked on my door very civilly. "Won't you tell me what you've been dreaming together? I believe you now. Please tell me."

I sighed, and let her in.

Chapter Nine

We were on a luminous white beach at dawn again. We smiled at each other, and ran back to the entrance of the cave where the ocean broke in arching tongues at the open darkness of its mouth. We stood irresistibly kissing on the rocks for a while before taking refuge inside, laughing, soaking wet and shivering with cold, but we soon took care of that by putting our minds together like two pieces of wood and imagining a fire into life. Its red flames licked up out of the shadows like the tongues of hungry little animals desperate for the nourishment of our appreciation. We knelt beside them, holding our palms over the fire, and it seemed to rise up out of the pleasure we took in its energetic warmth. I can't really explain it, but that's how it was. Our cold wet flesh and the hot dry flames were both part of us, as if we ourselves had created contrasts for the pleasure of sensation. We glanced toward the interior of the cave knowing that wonders awaited us, each gleam of gold in the ebony walls the encapsulated dawn of an unknown world that – with the consciously sharp picks of our thoughts and the driving force of our desires – we could pull out of the void of space so its jagged luminosity became the rays of a sun rising over the open field of our palms as the realm of a new dream came into being ruled by our awareness and fertilized by our creativity. Then, after we lived in it for as long as we found it exciting, the world we had enjoyed would fall like a golden leaf onto the royal necklace worn by the bodies of our eternal spirits...

The pull into the rich darkness of the endless interior of the cave was very strong, but that night we were more into staring at each other with the powerfully arousing knowledge that we were sleeping and yet acutely conscious, alone in our flesh and yet together in our feelings, our two bodies the living heart of the dream irresistibly drawn to each other like the two parts of the single beat that defines life. I knew then, viscerally and not just conceptually, that if it wasn't for love the world around us would not exist in the same way that life ends when the heart ceases the haunting duality of its rhythm. He grasped my hands and led me over to the violet towel lying across the sand.

He made me rest comfortably on my back across it, and I moaned, suffering a mixed thrill of awe and dread as he crouched between my legs and his golden head set between them. I was afraid of just lying there like a cold fish while his tongue dove determinedly in and out of me in between concentrating on the elusive pearl of my clit. I should have known that being eaten out in a dream by my dream man would be an entirely different and utterly overwhelming experience. The violet towel beneath me was vibrating like a live frequency flowing through my own flesh as the hot shaft of two of his fingers opened me up, the balls of his talented digits pressing into the receptively tender channel of my pussy creating silent chords sending beautifully sharp notes of pleasure singing through my blood which was itself a pure, sparkling energy. His twirling tongue and thrusting fingers had me whimpering and clutching the bottomless sand as I both suffered and gloried in a rush of sensations indistinguishable from images... I saw whirlpools and shafts of sunlight, cosmic circles and infinite right angles as everything added up to a finer and finer ecstasy taking me higher and higher even as it carved itself deeper and deeper into the dark core of my being which was slowly, magically disintegrating like a seed... until I wasn't aware of anything as I exploded completely into myself, blinded by the beauty of my true nature as Alex ravenously devoured the lavishly perfumed petals of my labia, growling with satisfaction as I climaxed into his mouth.

The dream became deliciously normal as he spread himself on top of me and I happily welcomed his hard cock into my slick deep need for him. I felt as carefree as one of my old Barbie dolls knowing that the unbound force experiencing itself through her has everything wonderfully under control... I was both the mortally stiff doll and the eternal child bent over her game in the living curve of the sky, Weeping Willows the soft fall of my hair caressing toy tombstones...

"Wait," Alex whispered. "I want to stay here for a while."

I opened my eyes, returning to the amazingly real space of our cave and the shelter of his arms. "I'm sorry." I smiled. "I just got to thinking..."

"Well, don't think anymore, I want you to be right here with me... I want to tell you something clearly and not go off on a rollercoaster of images. Are you keeping your mind perfectly blank?"

"Yes, sir."

"We can't be together like this anymore," he announced.

'What?" I gasped.

"Please, Isabel, try to understand... I should be dreaming with my wife like this."

"Oh, God." I was suddenly so numb with misery that I lost my hold on the dream's delicate reins, his warmth receding as I began waking up.

"No!" I felt his whisper like a fresh breeze blowing into the space of my consciousness which had been instantly hollowed out and rendered lifeless with sadness, the remains of my beautiful beliefs ghostly spider webs. "Stay with me, Isabel!" The depressing webs disintegrated beneath the warm force of his breath. "Don't go yet, listen to me, please..." I returned to the dream and his eyes looking down into mine again. "I think I'm falling in love with you," he confessed, "and it's got to stop before that happens." The roar of the ocean was in my ears, I was fully in the grip of his arms and the dream again. "Please try and understand." There was such a depth of sadness in his eyes that I was afraid of drowning in them with the weight of my love for him, needing the mysterious vessel of his smile to stay afloat. "Do you understand?"

"No," I replied, "because I love you already... and it isn't fair, she already has you in real life so why can't I have you in dreams?"

"Because they're one and the same thing, don't you see?"

"Yes." He was right, of course, but I had hoped he would end up wanting to live his real life with me, not start dreaming with his wife. "But why can't you love both of us?" I asked desperately. "If I'm willing to share you, why isn't she?"

"You know you're just saying that, Isabel."

"I know, but I'll do anything to keep dreaming with you."

"It's not right," he said without conviction, and this made me push him off me angrily. I leapt to my feet, glancing down at his startled form beginning to wake up, his flesh slowly merging with the twilight sky as I ran deeper into the cave. 'You're coming with me, Alex, whether you like it or not', I heard myself think as my room opened up coldly around me like the lifeless confines of a Barbie case into which I had been placed for a temporary pause in the game my higher powers were playing. I was trembling, and my limbs felt cold as a plastic doll's as I started crying at the thought that it was all over. Yet part of me knew everything had only just begun, somehow, and since absolute misery is a little exhausting after a while, I sat up in bed and listened to this calm and collected part of me.

'He didn't say he didn't want to keep dreaming with me, he said it wasn't right... he said he was beginning to fall in love with me, and I ran into the cave feeling I was taking him with me as he merged with the twilight'... I thought about this hard, knowing there was a secret message contained in the images. 'His flesh is light and his spirit is the sensual force latent in darkness... I am now going to take him on a journey into his own powers...' I flung my sheets off even though it was freezing in my room, the heat always being turned down at night to keep the gas bill as low as possible, but I was so aroused I didn't feel the cold, or if I did it only served to excite me further. I spread my legs, imagining our dream cave opening up between them and becoming deeper and deeper for his exploration...

'He's the only one for me... I don't know why, he just is, and I'm not going to let him get away, he's too deep inside me already... besides, he likes it there; he's having loads of fun, and now I'm going to start giving him more excitement than he can handle. Just you wait until tomorrow night, Alex, just you wait'. I really had no idea what I had in store for him, but the darkness of the cave's interior possessed the arousing atmosphere of a theatre just before the movie begins, only a million times more intense.

Chapter Ten

I was a witch flying amidst big old trees at night. My shawl was black and delicate as singed moth's wings, but its intricate web was still whole; unharmed by the glaring light of reason that had ruled in the world for so long. The trees were my friends, hundreds of years old each one, and they were whispering his whereabouts to me as I hovered amongst them. I flapped my arms gently up and down like a bird, my body parallel with the ground, smiling as I gazed down and around me. I spotted Alex's silver-black trunk and circled it slowly, amused to notice natural steps had formed in the bark, and that on the other side it extended smoothly down like a slide in a playground. I gripped the rough railing and climbed to the top, a little afraid because I was up so high and I was still a little dubious about my newfound power to fly. I stared down the silvery length of the tree, smooth as a ray of moonlight.

He wanted to forget me; he wanted me to slip out of his life, but his awareness had sprouted a whole new sense of possibility through contact with me. His thoughts were as mysteriously visible to me as branches silhouetted against the mirror of the full moon through which he was reflecting on his immortality, the opposite of the earthly mirror in which you see only your limits and inevitable decay. He knew now that his dreams were of his own making, so it followed then that his life was, too. He was certain of it now, the branches were telling me this clearly as sentences written in black ink on the page of the moon, and I was the "witch" who had broken the painfully limiting spell of his mortality. 'But it doesn't mean you have any claim on him', the tree silently communicated to me my own thoughts, and I started to fly around it to see if I could get around this fact by doing so, but there was no way I could, so I headed in the direction that a limb – separated from the rest of the tree by a bolt of lightning – was conspiratorially pointing me.

I flew into a clearing and came upon a large house similar to the Mansion through which I had consciously entered my dreams but much smaller, the toy version of it, and I abruptly realized I was in the past. This was not the twenty-first century; I could feel it in the relaxed way the earth was spread out around me and in the easy breath of the night; there were no choking some stacks anywhere in the distance. 'Oh, wild,' I thought, 'where am I'? I flew towards the house, enjoying the effortless undulation of my arms even though they weren't what was keeping me in the air. It was my own belief that I could rise above the ground and float around more conveniently and enjoyably that enabled me to fly. I had a body, yet I was purely my awareness and, therefore, light as a feather if I so chose. 'I could probably turn myself into a cat', I thought, cruising over the black pyramid of the roof. 'Or I could morph into a crow and fly onto a windowsill without attracting attention'. And just as I imagined this my shawl became two glossy black wings shining beneath the moon. I could see to my left and to my right but not before me, yet otherwise

I had the same conscious sense of myself, only with a different perceptive angle on the world.

Now I could eavesdrop without attracting attention, so I promptly flew towards the lighted window in an upper story of the house. I landed effortlessly on the sill and with my right eye peered into the room as my left eye gazed out at the dark, rustling mass of the forest. I was distracted from the scene inside sensing how full of life the trees and the ground were; they were positively writhing with it, the burrowing sound of worms like the static of a massive speaker system; electrical sparks filling the darkness. 'It's interesting being a bird', I thought. The dim space of the room didn't have much appeal, but a gleam of gold caught my eye and I realized it was his head, the soft strands of his hair the beloved nest of my soul. And his hair was gloriously long, worn in the fashion of a by-gone century, usually tied back but let loose now in the privacy of his bedroom. Being a bird was no longer an appealing circumstance, so I turned into a black kitten perched precariously on the sill, meowing anxiously for his attention. But apparently he couldn't hear me over the crackling of the fire and the silent weight of his own thoughts. He was bent over a small wooden desk writing something with a quill, the feather quivering with the sensual joy of being held in his hand. Then it slowly dawned on me where I was even though I had no idea how I knew. I was in the lifetime when he was beheaded during the French Revolution.

I scratched the windowpane urgently, and he turned his head. I put everything into a screaming "Meow!" and he stood up, brushing his hair away from his face in an exhausted gesture that almost killed me it was so noble and elegant. He quickly approached the window, and I realized he had finally seen me. He unlatched it, and pulled me inside with such humane swiftness that I went ecstatically limp.

"Poor little pussycat," he murmured, setting me down in front of the fire, almost as large as a burning forest to me in my kitten's form. "How did you get out there, little one?" His large, warm hand was a blissfully crushing weight as he stroked me, and it was a pleasure to hear myself purring. It seemed like a much nicer way to communicate how I felt about him than wrapping it up in words for his mind to chew on; this way my feeling merged directly with his and there was no need for any conceptual digestion. We were perfectly happy for a while with him petting me as I rolled onto my back, and then rubbed my cheeks against his fingers, wallowing in the warm world of his hands, until he remembered his problems and straightened up, abandoning me in favor of his desk again. I gazed at him sadly where I sat on the flagstones, motionless as an ancient Egyptian statue, wondering how I could help him. 'I can't, unless I turn into a woman', I thought, promptly curling up and taking human form again.

"You're probably hungry, aren't you?" he addressed me absently, and stretched his left arm toward a satin cord hanging between the desk and his canopy bed even as he kept writing.

"No," I said quickly, not wanting the intrusion of a servant.

He dropped his quill, turning very slowly in his chair to face me.

I was mad at myself for frightening him. "I'm sorry," I said, sitting up and noticing the long, clinging black dress I was wearing – supernaturally the organic remnants of my sleek black kitten's body.

"My Lord Jesus Christ!" he breathed.

"Yes, thanks to Him I'm not a vampire." I don't know why I said that, except that it seemed like a nice, natural way to start a theoretically impossible conversation. He just stared at me, his eyes as wide as a boy's, excited incredulity and reasonable disbelief battling each other to the death beneath their blue skies because he obviously didn't know he was dreaming or recognize me.

He stood up slowly. "I did not think I was a coward, yet I must be delirious with fear." He was talking to himself, and I felt he expected me to vanish as he approached me, but I didn't, so he paused uncertainly. Then a sudden anger flashed in his eyes. "I have no intention of selling my soul for a chance to continue living. My soul is all that is truly mine, therefore be gone, Satan!" He made a shooing gesture with his arm.

"I have nothing to do with that ridiculous bore of a creation," I corrected him politely. "I am a woman who loves you and is visiting you in a dream from the future, because everything you have felt is important to me; your feeling is the world through me, timeless and eternal."

"Is it you, Lucina?" he breathed, and a wave of memories hit me like a stack of cards falling one after the other picturing the events of my life… the violet dress I had seen myself wearing in another dream as he raised my hand to his lips; a villa in the Spring, the colorful flowers mirroring the women's dresses as they strolled across the lawns, the huge, inverted tulip buds of their skirts, and his velvet jacket the deep green of moss where he waited for me away from the others at the edge of the forest; the cruel blow of my betrothal to someone else, the clear pool in the garden filled as if with my own tears reflecting a pale, evanescent face and raven-black hair curling stubbornly, the power of my emotions refusing to obey the convenient, straight course of the life planned for them; and finally the even crueler, though less painful, blow of the guillotine blade flashing in the bright morning light.

'Oh, my, I'm dead, aren't I'? I was a little upset for a moment, but then I realized I was glad to be out of that ridiculous dress and all the frustrations symbolized by it – layers and layers of artificial obligations weighing me down. I sighed with relief. It was nice being dead and dreaming in the present rather than being stuck in time. Backstage is always much more delightfully fluid than the rigid script of the performance. "Yes, it is I, Lucina," I responded at last, pleased to don that personality again in order to re-experience its unique mood.

"*Lucina*!" he whispered, but didn't move any closer to me, apparently still worried I was a demonic apparition.

"Yes, it is me, Alex, do not be afraid."

"Alex? You are not she! Be gone, Satan!" He repeated that annoying shooing gesture and I suppressed a yawn of boredom, the purpose of this dream now obvious to me. I had to acquaint his past identity with his present, dreaming self. After all, he couldn't just let all the lives he had lived float aimlessly around in the darkness; he had reached a point where he had to start identifying less with his roles and more with their divine author.

"Alex, it's Isabel... you're dreaming," I began tentatively.

He covered his face with his hands. "Oh, my, God, this is not happening..."

I rose, silently approaching him.

'When I open my eyes, I will see a little black kitten, because there are no such things as witches... I simply have not been eating or sleeping enough..."

I grasped his wrists, pulling his hands away from his face. He stood frozen with fear, but it slowly malted as he felt that I was real. I made him look into my eyes so he would see the subliminal flame in them that was my love for him. "Alex..." I whispered, my hands slipping into his. "You're dreaming... it's me, Isabel..."

"Lucina," he whispered stubbornly.

"Isabel."

"Lucina."

"Oh, who cares!" I kissed him.

He pulled his hands out of mine, backing away. "Be gone, Satan!"

I turned into a crow again and flapped angrily around the room for a few minutes because I had suffered a horrible desire to slap him and this got it out of my system, but when I swooped towards him again I saw that he was lying on the floor, passed out with terror. My small black body elongated quickly, pouring down like a liquid undulating into a woman's form again so I could kneel beside him. "Oh, Alex, I'm sorry." I caressed his cheek.

He opened his eyes. "Isabel... I told you we couldn't dream together again." He raised himself on his elbows, looking around him.

I frowned. "My name is Lucina." I liked his attitude towards her better.

'Where are we?"

"In the past," I sighed.

He looked at me. "I told you we had to stop meeting like this, Isabel..."

"You're not my daddy; I don't have to obey you." I pushed him back down. "Do you remember what happened before you passed out?" I added curiously.

"Yes, I went to bed." He reached up and caressed my hair like a kitten playing with teasing strings, easily forgetting he was displeased with me.

"No, you've been dreaming for a while now."

"I have?"

"Yes, try and remember," I urged.

"'Why should I? There's nothing agreeable in the thought of losing my head."

"You remembered."

"Yes... yes... Lucina." He gazed at me tenderly.

I bent down and kissed him again. "See, you've loved me for centuries," I whispered.

"No..."

"Yes!" I caressed his chest with one hand while the other one moved lower.

"Yes..." He closed his eyes.

I giggled as I struggled to divest him of all the strange clothes he was wearing, distracted by the roughly luxurious feel of fabrics such as my fingertips had never experienced. It was no cheap costume he was wearing; he was truly wound up in the feel of that particular time and place. "God," I murmured in frustration, "is this fluffy silliness what eventually became streamlined into the sleek business tie?"

"Mm, yes, I think so..." He curiously caressed the cravat as I freed him from it.

"The naked skin is timeless!" I said with feeling.

"Mm, yes, and I like yours better every time, Isabel. Come here, this is my last night on earth, you know, I'm to be beheaded in the morning."

"Do you have any last wishes?" I teased, slipping the head of his hardening dick safely between my lips.

His rigid silence was response enough.

Chapter Eleven

"Isabel, are you ready?" Jackie was at my door because, somehow or other, unbeknownst to me, I had agreed to go on a double date with her. Her boyfriend's roommate was new in town and as a consequence he didn't know any girls. I couldn't back out now, having forgotten all about it until the last minute, but as I got ready I amused myself with the thought that of all the pretty, perfectly normal and happy girls in the city, it was just his luck to blind date a frustrated witch. 'The poor guy won't know what hit him'. Jackie had assured me he was cute. She had stated it at least one-hundred times when she was trying to convince me to agree to the date, and the constant repetition of that word made my sexuality feel like a horse she was feeding one square little sugar cube after another.

"Oh, shut-up," I snapped. "What the hell is that supposed to mean anyway?"

"What do you mean what's it supposed to mean? He's cute, what do you think it means?"

"Yes," I calmed down, realizing that metaphysically I was dealing with a five-year-old and that it wasn't right to lose your temper with children, "but what do you mean by cute? That he's well proportioned, I assume."

She sighed, controlling her temper because she wanted me to agree to the date. "Yes, that's what I mean... you conceited intellectual bitch," she couldn't resist adding, but her tone was agreeable.

"Well, what about the way he moves? What about his outlook on life, because that determines the attractiveness of his gestures, depending on whether he's creative and positive or fearful and conformist, intelligent and funny or dumb and profit-oriented. An easy test is how he reacts to the word 'mystery'."

"Isabel, I think you should see a psychiatrist, but first I think you should go out with Mike, he might be good for you. He'll help you forget Alex, believe me."

She was unfortunately aware of the fact that I had not received a letter from him in over a month, since the dream in the cave saying what he had told me then – that we had to stop dreaming together but that he would write me again. This hopeful clause didn't fool me, however; I knew it was the end. I hadn't dreamed anything lately, which was a truly oppressive state of affairs for me, so much so that I agreed to this blind date and consciously told myself I would try and be a good girl and forget Alex so long as I didn't lose my dreaming powers as well. I was anxious to go to sleep that night, curious to see if I could succeed in fooling my own psyche, because deep down I knew that as long as I had conscious control of my dreams, I would continue to look for him in them.

* * *

"You're really beautiful, Isabel, did you know that?"

"No, I didn't, tell me about it.' I smiled, wondering how

the hell I had ended up alone in a cab with him when we had all started out together. It somehow happened after the last bar.

"So why don't you have a boyfriend?" The inevitable question, one
that makes me feel like I'm in a doctor's office getting my knee ham-
mered on and asked why it doesn't react like everyone else's.

"Because, I don't believe in them." Fortunately, we were on our way
to my place, where he would drop me off and proceed to his.

"What do you mean... you' re not gay, are you?"

"Do I look gay?" I smiled wickedly.

"No." Unfortunately, he took this as a come-on, because he slid
over towards me on the seat. "Not at all, it's just what you said... I
don't get it."

"Neither do I, it's just a fact."

He laughed. "You're strange, Isabel, but I like you."

"Thanks." I looked out the window.

"You've had something on your mind all night," he observed, hoping to win me over with his sensitive perception of my mood, and his
alleged understanding of whatever might be wrong with me as he
silently waited for me to tell him.

"Yep." I chewed my gum contentedly, enjoying the dragon scales of
lights on the freeway beyond ours. Then I noticed my face faintly
reflected in the glass looking sad and bored as it flew through the sky,
stuck in the limits of this life as my image was in the frame of the window. What would happen when death shattered it? Would I finally be
free as myself completely, so that my inner life was the outer world as
well somehow, or would I just vanish?

"Do you want to tell me about it?" he insisted.

"No."

"Okay." He was offended.

"I'm sorry... you're a great guy, Mike, but take my word for it, I'm way too strange for you."

He laughed. "No you're not, you just think you are, but we're all strange in our own way. I think you're a very nice girl and I'd like to go out with you again, if that's all right with you."

I sighed. "I'm going to say a word, and you tell me the first thing that comes to your mind, okay?"

"Okay." He laughed again happily, thinking this was my weird way of casually accepting his invitation.

"Mystery."

"Sherlock Holmes."

"I thought so."

"What do you mean? Is there a right answer? What did you expect me to say?"

"Nothing." I leapt out of the cab almost before it had come to a stop. "Good night, Mike. Have a great life."

* * *

I was a governess in a French Manor, and, naturally, I was in love with the Lord. 'Oh, Christ, I'm not in some morbid Jane Eyre fantasy, am I? I want out of this dream now, please'. But the door in the wall of my small bedroom led into the winding corridors of a lifetime's unique plot, not into the freedom of my waking self. Yet after a moment, since I somehow knew Alex was one of the characters, I picked up the shawl lying across a chair and donned my role, becoming instantly wrapped up in its emotions as the intricate weave on the cloth draped over my shoulders.

I opened the door out into the hallway, and with the rush of cool air (my room was kept pleasantly warm by a fire in the corner) came a stream of memories, intangible and invisible and yet utterly real; my soul experiencing them like my flesh did the sudden chill. I had been the governess of his seven-year-old son for over a year and his wife was stunningly beautiful, with full breasts and a radiant smile that gladdened even *my* heart. Alex hardly noticed me. 'I have to find a mirror', I thought, because I didn't like the feeling of looking like less than what I was, or what I knew I had become. There was an ornate monstrosity hanging on the wall over a small wooden table on which sat a silver candleholder. "Oh, my God!" I was the pale ghost of myself, as if I was looking at an earlier, less accomplished sketch of my present features, and I could already see the wrinkles where my spirit was crumbling this version as casually as a piece of paper, preparing to throw it into the wastebasket of the grave to begin the full-color painting from the skeletal base of this life and what I had learned in it. I wasn't ugly; that was still me somehow, just a little washed out and undefined, and I liked the soft brown curls around my neck. 'I wonder what *he* looks like here'… I turned away from the mirror and suddenly had the strangest experience. I saw the narrow hallway extending to my left and to my right as the frail thread of a spider's web alive inside my mind; as a quivering filament of light inside the awareness of my soul spinning the memory of this life around me again. I walked slowly down the dark-red carpet with the sense of being a single cell in the vast body of all my lives, yet also half a beat of their mysterious heart, of which the other half was always him. Yet I knew that in this life we had never truly been together. I knew then that I had pined away with love for him, just as I was foolishly doing in my present incarnation. 'That was the mistake,' I thought, 'I have to *make* him love me. So what am I doing as a shy little governess'? And suddenly I remembered the band of gypsy's that used to camp out just beyond the Manor grounds during the summer. I always secretly envied them their freedom, even though it frightened me, especially when I saw the way Alex looked at one of the young women when she came to the door for some reason or other, I think to ask for a doctor for her baby after all her herbal remedies had failed. 'I'll be back', I determined, 'and this time it won't be my baby who's sick, it'll be me'.

At the end of the hall there was a floor-length glass window through which the sun slowly began to shine as though it faced the eastern horizon and a normal day was dawning. I ran towards it and crashed through the glass, my dress and shawl disintegrating like burning moth's wings around me. I was free, flying down to the fresh green lawn in the form of a butterfly, the all-embracing light coalescing and dimming into the open heart of the flower I landed on. Then my wings opened and became a gypsy's colorful skirt spread out across the grass of a timeless morning.

Chapter Twelve

I saw the lights in the Manor going on amidst the leaves. My deepest self said, 'Sorcery is evil'! while my desire cried, 'I want him'! I had accidentally wandered onto the Manor grounds while he was out hunting and his hounds had chased after me. I ran swift as a cat through the trees, dumb with terror, only finding my voice to scream when one of the dogs tore my skirt and the other one bit my ankle. I remember hearing his voice commanding them to release me, and the sound was as blessed to me as the divine voice of an angel calling off the hounds of hell. Then everything went black as I fell, the sweet, safe earth of my grave engulfing me, freeing me from all fear and pain… I died that day, because when I opened my eyes again he was staring down at me and I was in heaven, his golden hair a shining halo of light, his eyes the vivid blue of a summer sky. I knew without a doubt in my heart that he was the angel who had smiled over my birth and whose lips were the horizon of my life, the rising and setting sun the dimples of his pleasure.

"It seems you have caught a woman instead of a hare or a fox," I heard myself say. "Are you disappointed, my Lord?"

"Have they hurt you?" He ignored my question, looking away from my face down to my ankle.

"Yes." I saw I was bleeding, but I knew from the little pain I felt that my skin was only scratched.

"If you had not left your people's camp and wandered onto my land my dogs would not have chased after you," he scolded me absently, kindly, and I noticed he was gazing at the slender brown curve of my leg visible through the tear in my skirt and not at my wound.

"Forgive me, my Lord, I have learned my lesson... pain is a good teacher." I fell back across the grass, but it was swiftly growing desire for him – mingled with the fear that it might be impossible to fulfill – that caused my sudden weakness. "Oh..." I moaned.

"They have hurt you." He lifted me quickly but gently up into his strong arms.

"No," I murmured. 'Where are you taking me? Please do not punish me, my Lord. I did not realize I had walked so far..."

"I am taking you to my home where you will be looked after until you are well."

"You are too kind, my Lord."

Needless to say, it caused quite a scandal when he rode up with a gypsy in his saddle. I had pretended to faint so I could rest my head on his shoulder, and I decided it was the best condition to remain in; putting him in the position of defending me and thus himself since I had become a mysteriously silent part of him. I heard the anxious voices of servants shouting, and then the preemptory tone of the woman I assumed was the main housekeeper.

"Think of your wife, Lord Wolfson," she said. "You cannot insult her by bringing this... this creature into her house. There is fresh hay in the barn..."

"You will make a room ready for her, Anna, with a hot bath, and cut up a linen sheet for bandages. My dogs have mauled her and she will remain in my home until she is able to leave it without assistance."

'Which will be never', I thought, moaning as if in deep pain, but really because I had almost smiled.

I felt him carry me upstairs into a room and spread me across an unbelievably comfortable bed. "Now be gentle with her, Anna, she has a soul even if it is not as virtuous as your own." He was teasing her, and I heard the woman make a gruff, affectionate sound. I opened my eyes for a second, and his smile made me think of an angel again. I writhed jealously. 'Soon he will smile only for me, only for me', I thought. 'His hair will shine beneath my hands and no one else's'.

When I knew I was alone with Anna, I opened my eyes, and their raven-black depths immediately made her cross herself and glance at the door as if to call her master back for protection. But silently, with tight lips and averted eyes, she obeyed his instructions by bathing and bandaging my ankle as I stared at her.

"Nothing, only a few scratches!" she said contemptuously. "You could have walked *in* without assistance."

"Perhaps I have bewitched your Lord," I suggested with a secret smile.

She laughed, and her relaxed amusement enraged me. "Lord Wolfson's virtue is well beyond the reach of your heathen spells. The only thing that can enchant him is his wife's smile, and it has been that way for over twenty years."

"Then she is already in the autumn of her life. Soon a frost of white hairs will strike her brow, and bird's claws will mark the corners of her eyes as her youthful flame deserts her and she begins to warm herself by the fire of memory while her husband, still in the hot summer of his manhood, lies elsewhere."

She slapped me. "Your wound is bandaged. Now leave before I have you thrown out."

"I will not." I smiled, provoking her.

"Get out, you filthy gypsy!" She was flushing a hot red that made her wide face look like an overripe tomato, so that I knew my next remark would make her burst into a paroxysm of emotion.

"Have you never thought that perhaps his name reveals his secret soul?" I suggested. "He is Lord of the wolves, Anna, because in love he is as fierce as one."

"Get out!" She reached for me, but I rolled over to the other side of the bed just as I heard the bedroom door open. I quickly began crying.

"Anna, what have you been saying to her? I asked you to tend to her wounds, not to inflict new ones with your sharp tongue!"

"Lord Wolfson..." She could barely breathe she was so angry. "It is not I... not I!" she gasped. "The things she said... she told me she had cast a spell on you!"

I sobbed, shaking my head slowly from side to side, as if I had heard this so many times before I was dangerously close to dying of weariness.

"Please leave us, Anna." He was angry, and I dared to look at him then through the black strands of my hair, acting like a frightened kitten cruelly trapped in the cage of an ignorant serving woman's superstitions.

"But my Lord…"

"Leave us, Anna."

I scrambled quickly off the bed. "No, my Lord, it is I who should leave. First I trespass on your grounds and ruin the pleasure of your hunt, and now I bring discord to your household." I limped towards the door.

He gently grasped my arm and led me back over to the bed. "It would please me if you would stay here for the night, until the shock of what has happened has passed in a restful sleep, and in the morning I will take you back to your people."

"She is worse than a lazy, stealing gypsy," Anna declared abruptly, "she is a witch!" She crossed herself and left the room.

'Why does she hate me?" I looked up into his eyes, knowing the intense desire I was experiencing for him, but painfully could not give into, made them shine with the ghost of tears.

He grasped my shoulders, making me lie back across the bed. "She is an old woman who has heard too many tales by the kitchen fire. Do not let her upset you. I will have another servant bring you a tray of food, and a glass of wine to warm your heart to this room that is your home for the night…"

I grasped his hand and kissed it, letting go of it quickly, as if it would burn me to hold it any longer.

"…And where nothing can hurt you," he finished what he had been saying after hesitating a heartbeat, as though the feel of my lips had distracted him, and I was filled with joy to know that I had almost made him forget what he was saying.

"You are too kind, my Lord." I closed my eyes.

* * *

I enjoyed my meal and my wine as I thought of the morning when I would feel him against me on the saddle again, but this time I would be awake and directing him to a secret place I knew of where no one would disturb us. As I was stripping for the luxury of sleeping in a real bed stuffed with feathers, I became weak with longing at the thought that he might come to me in the darkness when the household was asleep. I imagined the door opening slowly, and the powerful silhouette of his form approaching me, and the dissolving warmth of his breath as he whispered to me not to be afraid... but the next thing I knew the sun was blinding me, followed by fury when I discovered that Lord Wolfson had sent a steward to escort me home. So there I was, gazing at the Manor through the branches of trees in those moments just after twilight when I felt the full weight of my desire in my heart burning like the dying sun and sending a surge of impatience through my blood. I had many lovers, but none of them cooled my longing for him; they only made it worse. Men were as numerous as the waves of the sea, but letting them possess me to try and forget him was like drinking a cup of salt water; I felt like retching afterwards and my lust for him became even more intense; my heart a flaming iron in the shape of his name branding me his eternal possession against my will...

"Isabel, get up. You're late."

I woke to my present life, and it felt very strange suddenly seeing the open space of my room littered with the colorful tights I wore to exercise like an open box under a Christmas tree, but not a normal tree, to be sure – a massive dark Evergreen filling the universe decorated with the lights of stars and the colorful balls of planets. Because in this lifetime I had opened the gift of magical awareness, all my other incarnations were strewn around me like dolls I could consciously grasp and become one with again. I could easily see now beyond my own mortal borders as the spirit that had fashioned all my lifetimes in the mysteriously enjoyable process of experience and growth.

"Get up, Isabel!"

"I'm up," I groaned. I was going to work in an office, but my emotions were still with my bohemian gypsy self dying of love for Lord Wolfson, who was really Alex. The parallels with this lifetime were obvious. 'She's going to try sorcery on him, the silly fool... but isn't trying to be with him in the realm of dreams a form of sorcery as well? I'm seeking to win his love with this strange power I possess, and that his wife doesn't, to intersect with his soul in another dimension and join my imagination with his like two bodies making love, our ideas like limbs entwining... it *is* sorcery'. I felt terrible, but as I left the house the pure blanket of snow covering the world for some reason reassured and comforted me. 'My love for him has to be this pure and selfless or else it's not love, only lust. The gypsy wanted to please his flesh, sensing he was not strong enough to resist her if she persevered, but his body is the part of him that worms dine on in the end and it was his love for his wife that fed the dignity of his soul. I trapped him in the carrion embrace of the earth with my lust. I destroyed his self-respect, his peace of mind, and thus his connection with his spirit. He was no longer virtuously secure of his immortality after he became murderously stained with the blood of his wife's heart'.

I was very subdued at work that day, almost cringing when the married men in my office flirted with me in their usual innocent

way. 'Alex was right, it was wrong for us to keep dreaming together. Just because we didn't have corruptible bodies didn't make it
right'. I wondered if I would return to that lifetime as a gypsy
tonight, part of me hoping I would, because now that I knew my
behavior had been wrong it was safe to enjoy again all the fun I had
had corrupting him. Then I realized what I was thinking. 'Isabel,
you're a hypocrite. You'd do best to remember being a nun and
dream about that a few nights as penance'. And this thought made
me wonder about the fact that so far I had experienced Alex only as
a rich man who looked very much like he did now. 'Aha, proof that
you're making all this up because if you weren't he would have
been poor and ugly in another incarnation... But why should I
remember those lifetimes? I can't recall things that happened when
I was a baby... maybe less developed selves are to the soul what
early childhood is to a mortal adult, obscure and very basic, when
you're learning elementary physical lessons, and the lives you
remember are the one's where your profound awareness of self was
beginning to develop... he was beheaded in that other life time and
so was I, so it's not like I'm being idyllic, and in this one I ended up
corrupting him and destroying his happiness and ruining his old
age. If I was imagining it, that certainly wouldn't have been what
happened'.

I got home, later than usual because the Red Line out to Dorchester
was always delayed on snowy days, but I hadn't even noticed the trip; I
was still lost somewhere in a forest gazing up at the windows of his
Manor House. 'I know it was wrong, but, seeing as I'm being good
now, can't I experience the pleasure of corrupting him just once more'?
I lit my last violet candle. 'This is it, baby, this is goodbye, because my

love for you is sacred and good, but desire and possessiveness are bad and for the worms'…

His windows were lit and the night was heavy on my soul because I could not feel the weight of his body on mine. "I will die if he does not take me! I will die!" My aunt knew how I felt and told me there were ways to win his love not known to normal women, and that she would share these secrets with me. "But you most be sure he is the one you want, because if you invoke the dark forces to bind him to you, you will never be rid of him."

"I want him for all eternity!"

"Then you must go to the glade of the oaks at midnight on the night of the full moon."

"What must I do there?"

"You most please the dark gods if you want them to grant you what you desire; you must endear them to you so they begin to grow angry at Lord Wolfson for making you unhappy."

"No, I do not wish to hurt him…"

"They will not hurt him because they know you desire him. Just as hunting dogs do not tear the skin of their master's prey but deliver it unharmed, so they will bring your Lord to you."

"Tell me what I must do!"

"You most lie upon the grass and slowly bring yourself to fulfillment with your eyes closed, so that demons will feel safe to gather around you and enjoy the pleasure that flows from you, because it is a source of power for them when there is not the body of a lover absorbing it from you. And all the time you must have his image in your mind and his name upon your lips, for though devils surround you, they cannot touch you while you call to him."

"Is that all I must do?"

"Yes, but there is danger, my child, for if during your climax you lose sight of his image and cease to whisper his name, the dark forces will enter your body and you will go mad."

"There is no danger of that. I cannot for one second forget him, even in the arms of other men."

"Then go to the glade on the night of the full moon and do as I said."

"But when will he come to me?"

"On the night of the new moon, after your spell is complete, jealous demons will enter his dreams and fill them with your image. They will be strong with the force of your lust and angry at him because your love for his soul barred them from entering your body and possessing you themselves."

"They will not hurt him?"

"No. They will lure him to you in the hope that once you have had him you will not desire him any more and they will be able to claim you."

"Demons are like children then, if they are so easily tricked."

"They are not children; they are adults who were so selfish and evil in life that their souls were blinded, and now they wander the night able to feel only the burning fire of lust kindled by living flesh; drawn to it like freezing beggars to a hearth. You will feel your heart pounding with fear in your breast as they surround you, so know it is their fists beating to be let into the warmth of your body as they long for another sight of the stars and the freedom of the spirit through your eyes."

"How terrible! Do they remain demons forever?"

"I do not know. Perhaps when they have roamed the darkness long enough the spark of their lost soul rekindles inside them from the friction of their suffering against the eternal tree of life, and they are reborn and given another chance to reach heaven."

"But is it not wrong then to invoke them?"

"Do you want this man?"

"Yes!"

"Does he desire you in the same way?"

"He would, if he was not afraid of hurting his wife, I am sure he would... if I could be around him every day, I know he would fall in love with me, but I can never see him."

"Then there is no other way."

Chapter Thirteen

I had thought the spell would be easy to cast, almost enjoyable, but I was afraid as I walked to the glade. I had never left camp alone at this hour and the complete silence and darkness were oppressive, for I could bring no light with me. "The moon and your love for him must be your only guides."

The leaves seemed to whisper to me so sinisterly that I was always at the point of turning back, but I didn't, keeping his face before my eyes the way it had looked when I opened them and saw him bent over me, the sun shining in his golden hair forming a halo around his head… At last I reached the glade, the trees surrounding it swaying gently as if underwater, their rustling leaves bathed in silver light. I kept my eyes turned up to the moon.

In the center of the open space, I slowly removed my bodice, offering it up to the sun's consort before solemnly discarding it. Then I spread myself back across the grass and her pale, lovely face receded as if she did not approve of what I was doing. 'But I love him! I need him'! I defended myself in my head, raising my skirt. My hands were cold and my body reluctant as a mule to be moved;

I could not become aroused. But finally, a delicate pleasure lapped between my legs when I closed my eyes and pictured his face. He smiled, and my back arched from a sudden rush of lust as I whispered his name, "My Lord Wolfson!" I became a little frightened then by the fact that calling to him was also an invitation to wolves. Without a fire, I had no protection from nocturnal predators, yet my unrequited desire for this man was as sharp and painful to my soul as an animal's teeth ripping savagely into my flesh... I continued defiantly caressing myself, stoking my courage by crushing my clitoris and forcing it to bloom as I became perversely excited by the possibility of a wolf stalking me, irresistibly drawn to the feast of my pussy. My breath caught as terror stabbed me to the quick, and yet I deliberately bunched my long skirt up around my waist and spread my legs as far as I could, completely exposing my sex to the unknown; opening myself up to all the dangerous forces embracing me in the night. The moon seemed to be watching me intently now, as though she mysteriously approved of my absolute submission to the impenetrable darkness of the forest. And the longer I lay there like a willing sacrifice, the more vulnerable I allowed myself to become, the better my caressing, thrusting fingers felt as if they belonged to someone, to something, else. The slick delicate sounds made by my juicing pussy relentlessly opened up and fucked were mysteriously louder than the profound silence as my pleasure intensified, deepening uncontrollably and perfuming the cool breeze that licked my inner thighs almost intimately, as if alive...

My climax was so powerful that I cried out wordlessly, barely remembering that I had to continue calling out his name. "Oh, my

Lord! My Lord Wolfson!" The darkness rang with my voice and throbbed with my body.

* * *

On the night of the new moon, just as my aunt had said he would, he came to me in the glade. I heard the muffled sound of his horse's hooves, then the animal's noble black head loomed into the glow of the fire I had kindled like a sculptured section of the living darkness around me. He dismounted quickly, and I ran towards him. He pushed me away from him so violently that I fell back across the grass, but this only intensified my desire for him as I stared up at him with a slavish devotion.

"Why do you torment me?" he demanded.

His voice seemed to penetrate me. I moaned, rising onto my hands and knees.

"Why?"

His passion was devastating me with joy. I began crawling towards him.

"I defended you against Anna when she called you a witch, and yet she was right. You *did* cast a spell on me. I find no peace in my bed. My wife's arms can no longer hold me. My soul is tormented by demons showing me what it would be like to possess you, a thousand different ways even though you mean nothing to me."

"Then why did you come here tonight?" I rose and stood proudly before him.

"To tell you that if you do not set me free, I will kill you." He rested his hand on the hilt of his dagger.

"Yes, please, kill me!" I knelt at his feet. "I did not want to do this, please believe me. I swear I did not. My aunt said it was the only way to cure myself of the love I felt for you. I did not know it was a spell I was casting. I thought I was freeing myself of you, because the thought of you haunts me when the sun is out and blinds me in the night. It is destroying me. So, yes, please, kill me. I can think of no greater joy than dying by your hand."

He drew his weapon and I lay back across the ground, raising my arms over my head and turning it away, joyfully waiting for his thrust without caring what form it took; not caring if I survived it, almost not wanting to.

I felt the cold point of his blade pierce the flesh over my heart. I held my breath, wanting either his knife or his cock to possess me, because either one was better than him riding away indifferently.

"Swear to remove the spell you have cast upon me." His voice was hoarse where he knelt over me.

'With desire or with anger'? I wondered, almost falling into a languid dream state inside the dream it was such bliss to feel my life in his hands. But I opened my eyes and gazed up at him. "It is you who have cast a spell on me, my Lord. I am your slave. Do with me as you will."

He leaned forward.

I gasped as blood flowed over my breast, its sinister red trickle the loose thread of a garment slowly unweaving it. But I kept gazing worshipfully up at him, his features harshly motionless in the pulsing firelight, his will battling my desire. "Kill me!" I breathed. "I love you."

He flung the dagger away abruptly.

"No, please kill me!" I sat up and handed the weapon back to him, He took it almost absently, staring at the wound he had inflicted in me, so that I knew he was beginning to believe in his own guilt. "You were right, my Lord, I was casting a spell on you because I love you, so you must kill me." I was compelled to tell him the truth even though I did not want to.

"No." He put his knife away, grasped my hands, and pulled me to my feet. "No," he repeated calmly. "You are young and cannot be blamed for your ignorance."

"Then you forgive me for being so horrible, my Lord; for invoking dark forces to win your love; for lying naked beneath the moon with your image in my mind and your name upon my lips, knowing the pain of solitary pleasure so the night would carry my longing into your dreams? I wish the wolves had stopped me. They should have defended their Lord."

"But if demons do not really exist, then why are my nights disturbed by dreams of you, sinful images that rage like a fire beneath my bed so that sleep becomes a torment and my wife's virtuous arms the ropes condemning a heretic?" He spoke quietly to himself, his eyes not seeing me.

"Demons do exist, and they have helped me cast a spell upon you, so you must kill me if you wish to be free." I unsheathed his dagger again stubbornly and slipped it back into his hand.

He stared into my eyes, which I knew were darker than the night, and his arm slipped around my waist, pulling me to him. "No," he whispered, "for if I kill you, then I will never be free of you."

I gazed up at him with trusting devotion.

"Do you have a name or should I just call you Witch?" He smiled coldly, but his body was warm and his sex was growing firm against my belly, weakening me so much that I could not even raise my own voice from out of my throat to respond. "It is just as I thought." His hold tightened and my arms slipped around his neck with the swift smoothness of serpents claiming him. "You have no name because you have no soul." I felt him raising the hand in which he held the dagger. "Which means that to kill you would not be a sin…"

"My name is Isabel!" I gasped, and the sudden light that came into his eyes subliminally transformed the rustling trees of the glade into a theatre curtain around the open space of a stage. I glanced around me, surprised, because only a very distant part of me had remembered I was dreaming, and Alex had not realized it at all.

"Isabel…" He glanced down at the knife in his hands. 'What…"

"Kill me, Alex!" I clung to him. "Please!"

"Are you crazy?"

"No, please, I know what I'm doing. It's your revenge. Take it." I let go of him, stepping beck, and from his expression I knew he saw the blood on my chest in the firelight.

"You're hurt…"

"Oh, Alex, don't be a fool and kill me. I deserve it." It was painfully clear to me that I was at a crossroad. I could do what I had done in the past and continue trying to seduce him into my dreams, or I could let him go. "You were a hell of a lot sexier as Lord Wolfson, Alex. He was about to kill me and I was totally into it, but now you're wimping out."

"Oh, am I?" He pulled me roughly to him again. The mention of his name seemed to bring it all back to him instantly.

"Yes. And you were so pathetically easy to seduce."

"That's because I could imagine doing things to you I never would have considered doing to my wife, who I respected, but you were like an animal crawling all over me…

"And you loved it."

"Yes, but I didn't love *you*. I wanted to kill you. You made me feel as though my soul was filled with red ants. And each time I imagined fucking you my guilt got heavier, until it turned into the stone of my grave because I couldn't take it anymore."

"And you're so weak that even though you know all this now you still can't kill me!"

He took a step back and thrust the dagger deep into my belly. I cried out beneath the sudden, controlled violence of his penetration, and the sensation of his absolute possession of me was so intensely fulfilling that describing it as either pain or pleasure became meaningless. He held me hard against his side, and pulled the dagger out of my womb just for the pleasure of thrusting the remorseless blade deeper and deeper into my body again and again and again...

I woke with my cries resounding in the dark room. The last violet candle was gone.

Chapter Fourteen

"Oh, yes, that feels so good, so good…" Mike's eyes were closed, his head rolling helplessly on the pillow while my tongue circled his penis, rising like a tower from the smooth plain of his body and easily conquered by me.

Satisfying him was as easy as saying my ABC's and just about as exciting. This was the first time we had slept together, and I already knew it was going to be the last. I was so bored the world felt like a vast yawn as God fell asleep, but not to dream.

"Oh, yes, yes, Isabel…"

I hated giving him head; I hated having his meaningless tower of flesh in my mouth, because I didn't love him so there was no soul I desired to capture and taste in the deliciously concentrated essence of his cum. When he ejaculated, I dutifully pumped his erection, but I didn't swallow; I kept my face turned away feeling existentially sick. I had given him a blowjob because I felt guilty and wanted to give him as much pleasure as possible before I never saw him again, and because I hadn't been able to respond to him as he tried in his overly eager, elementary way to arouse me. He sucked on my breasts like a starving baby, expecting me to take pleasure from his dog-like slobbering and pawing. He was about to penetrate me when I pushed him over onto his back. He was startled, but then I proceeded to devastate him with my mouth, grateful that at least he wasn't inside me pretending to possess me. He came quickly enough as I pumped him fiercely with my hand watching the volcanic explosion of sea foam.

"God, that was great!" he gasped. "Now it's my turn…"

"No." I smiled sweetly. "Aren't you hungry? Wouldn't you rather eat some food?"

He laughed. "You were right, you *are* strange, Isabel, but I definitely like you." He pulled me down into his arms before I could protest. "And you are *definitely* a nice girl, I knew you were."

I wished again that when I went to sleep that night that I would never wake up; that I would just fall into a dream and be with Alex forever. Even if he didn't realize he was dreaming, even if he didn't know me, at least I would be with him and pleasing him in any way I could.

"Come on, won't you let me?" Mike coaxed, sitting up and trying to spread my legs.

"No!" I whimpered like a virgin. I only wanted Alex inside me, in my dreams, in my body, only him.

"Why not?" he asked gently, and I could tell he was enjoying my resistance; it must have been arousingly different for him.

He was cute, and nice, and there was absolutely nothing wrong with him that I could see, except that he was… normal. "Because…" I answered, keeping my legs closed.

"Come on…" He clearly thought I was just making it more enjoyable to give in.

"Oh, Mike, I'm sorry, I'm in love with someone else, but he's married, so it's impossible."

My sudden confession hit him like a gunshot. "Oh." He fell onto his back.

"I'm sorry. It's not that I don't like you, you know I do, I just haven't been able to forget him yet."

"It's all right," he said, employing his usual tactic of winning me over with his amazing understanding.

"So why don't you help me forget and take me out to dinner and a movie?" I asked.

"Now?" He looked lazy and infuriatingly satisfied.

"Yes." I pouted.

"Okay, if that's what you you'd like." He was already warming to the idea, because at least in a movie he wouldn't have to deal with my strange personality, only the uncomplicated pleasure of holding my hand and being seen with a beautiful girl.

Jackie came in as we were leaving. "Hi, Mike." She grinned, and her silent glance in my direction was like a statement written in the code of lights flashing in her eyes: 'So, you've finally come to your senses'.

* * *

I did not fall into an enchanted sleep that night. I dreamed Mike was trying to go down on me, but my thighs were the banks of a river steel-gray with pollution and his tongue was a shuddering fish dying from the toxic waste of an empty pleasure...

I woke up more miserable than I had ever been in my life. I felt I would die, except that I could clearly see Alex's face in my mind's eye illuminating my inner darkness with a remembered joy that was indestructible. I kept a pen and a note pad by my bed, and since I didn't have anymore candles, I lifted the window shade and began writing by the glow of a streetlight.

LAMENT

Factory towers burning cancerous
Holes into my living green witch's cloak
Desires wrapped in fatal amniotic plastic
Dragon eyes burning at night over polluted moats

Experience is chained to assembly line scales
Deep feeling a vanishing sword of power
Rational doubts weak screws in the heart's dreaming armor
The soul's virginal wonder raped by the T.V. tower

The trees are being stripped for fashion magazines
A vestige of my soul in a black slip under studio lights
Like the glow of street lights in sordid city skies
The stars as invisible as penetrating thoughts in my eyes

Love's mysterious unfolding isn't really believed
The same old marketable climax without real feeling
Children growing up to realize that the hands of the clock
Point in a different direction than their mother's caressing
Into the world of dreams, her lips whispering
A fairytale under its ticking like the clanging
Of a still distant chain that is now all they feel

Jackie told me there was an article on Alex's band in a certain magazine, so on my way back from work I stopped by a bookstore and bought it. I didn't really want to; I felt the glossy plastic burning my palms like dry ice. 'Why do I want all this information on him? It's only going to make me love him even more'. I felt like a pigeon accepting the crumbs of these general public facts in order not to starve. I read the brief article on the train, trying not to look at his picture.

I found out that he painted, and this fact successfully devastated me for the rest of the week wondering what his work looked like; wondering if some of our dreams had found their way into his art. I also read that he spent a good deal of his money on clothes. According to the article, he never wore the same outfit twice. I was pondering whether or not to think him vain and superficial because of this, desperate for any excuse not to love him so much.

The following morning was Saturday, and even though life was meaningless and I was completely miserable, at least I didn't have to go to work. I could enjoy reclining on the depth of my depression and the illusion that there was something profoundly erotic about it; open to the caress of circumstances in the hope that someone might come along and turn this inert existentialism into creative ecstasy. The weekend provided a free, open space in which I felt something unexpected and exciting could happen, whereas the weekdays followed a fixed schedule I didn't have enough time and energy to deviate from. 'Routine is like a snake, it makes things run smoothly, but your soul starts to go numb from the deadly venom of improbability and boredom it slowly injects into your blood', I thought morbidly.

"Did you read the article?" Jackie asked when she saw me lying as if at my own wake on the couch. She was on her way out. "Did you read about all his clothes? He's probably really conceited, and he's so fucking busy, besides being married. I can't see why you're so obsessed with him, he's not even that cute. You're not still thinking about him, are you? What happened with Mike? Did you go out with him again? Say something."

"No."

"No *what*?"

"No, I didn't go out with Mike again and I never will, unless the body snatchers get me. And no, Alex is not conceited; he's just symbolically expressing the enjoyable, incarnating power of his higher being which changes bodies like he does outfits. And yes, I'm still thinking about him, and you're right, he's not cute, he's beautiful."

"Isabel, you have to try and forget him and live your own life."

To my utter amazement she came and sat beside me like my mother used to when she saw I was sad. She gazed down at me with a genuine concern that made tears of self-pity spring to my eyes it was so wonderfully unexpected.

"I can't," I said desperately, turning onto my side and burying my face in a cushion.

"He's an asshole! Here he has this incredible experience with you, dreaming with you and then meeting you in real life, and it's nothing to him!"

"That's not true…"

"Oh, come on, Isabel, face it, he's spoiled by fame and fortune, and dreaming with you was just another pleasure thrown his way for being a precious rock star. You think he's really deep and intense, but you're just projecting your own feelings on him. He's no more special than someone like Mike, who's a really hot bass player and might just make it into the big time himself."

"Jackie, are you insinuating I'm a stupid little groupie dazzled by riches and the god-like phallus of a guitar?"

"No, I know you're not stupid, but you do strike me as a little immature. You're not sixteen, it's time you became a little more realistic about life and love…"

"Jackie, are you forgetting Alex and I actually did meet in dreams before we met in so-called real life?"

"No…"

"Then you're going to have to define what you mean by realistic."

"Oh, forget it!" She became Jackie again and I closed my eyes with relief as she got up to go. "You're impossible. If you want to be miserable, go right ahead. But if you want to know my honest opinion, I think you're a goddamned idiot. Any girl in her right mind would go for Mike."

"Well, that explains it, because I'm in my left mind. I appreciate your concern, though, and I am trying to forget about him, I just don't know how I possibly can…"

"Call Mike; I hate telling him you're not here or that you're in the shower. He'll help you forget."

I sighed. "No."

"All right, pine away, it's your life you're wasting!" She slammed the front door behind her.

It was a relief to see her go so that I could stop defending my heart like a castle from the relentless siege of her reasoning. What I felt for Alex was what made life worth living, and that was all there was to it. The thought of him was the lightning bolt of joy that brought me to life, the miraculous machinery of my body a dead weight without the animating force of my love for him. I had turned on the TV and was watching the re-runs of the series, *COSMOS*, and after a while I couldn't wait for Jackie to come home; growing so desperate for human interaction that I felt willing to temporarily limit the range of my perceptions. 'Oh, how nice it would be to want only the things she wants. Why do I have to have such a cosmically expanded sexual organ? My vagina only takes up a few inches; it's not the whole universe. Grow up… or down, actually… No, I can't, how I feel is how I feel'.

I turned Carl off and started cleaning the apartment. Jackie would appreciate it; it was my way of apologizing to her for not being normal. I had been living there alone, but when the landlord raised the rent, I was forced to look for a roommate. I suppose I had seemed likeable enough to her when she came for the interview. Poor girl, I had felt as guilty as a vampire fooling a mortal. It wasn't long before she was looking at me with confusion, wondering who the hell she had agreed to live with.

I finished my peace offering and found myself confronted with the impossible thought of Alex again. 'Oh, God, I can't, I can't stand it. I want him! I want the magic of my dreams, and it's not fair that they depend on my love for him'!

The phone rang.

"Dracula' s castle," I answered.

"Hi, it's Jackie. I just met the answer to all your problems. Steve and I are coming over with him later. His name's Ray, and he's their new lead singer. Wait till you meet him, he talks just like you!"

"Jackie…"

"Shut-up and look good. We'll be there at eight." She hung up.

* * *

Dressing up is always fun, even if you don't believe in what you're doing it for, because just knowing the sight of you is like a laser beam knocking all healthy men off their feet is fulfilling enough in itself. I was pleased with my little apartment, neat as a doll's house, and I wandered around it smug as a cat for a while sipping red wine and eating a piece of cheese.

Oh, I was inspired awaiting the answer to all my problems that I didn't for one second believe in. At seven-thirty, I went and stood in front of a mirror. 'You're a fool', I thought.

It was a month since Alex, as Lord Wolfson, had killed me.

* * *

"Did you tell him about my dreaming with Alex? He keeps looking at me weird." Jackie and I were having a quiet conference in the kitchen. I hadn't been prepared for this. I had expected to be able to treat her solution to all my problems as a joke, confident as a princess in her tower expecting a foolishly daring archer who would shoot the usual questions and comments at her. But Ray was like his name, disarmingly intense and direct. He brought fresh leaves into the apartment in his green eyes, but they were narrow, almost sinister.

"Yes, I did, he thought it was awesome and said he wanted to meet you. He believes in all the stuff you do, the soul, and the magic of creativity, and all that."

"Really?"

"Yes. He's hot, isn't he?"

Ray and Steve were waiting for us in the living room, having their own little conference, I could tell by the way Steve cleared his throat and smiled when we returned. I thought he was immature and very much appreciated Ray's almost indifferent sideways glance as he contentedly sipped his wine. He had such a gracious, sensual air of being perfectly fulfilled, but only for the moment, because there was also a hungry aura about him I liked in the nervous way I would have enjoyed seeing a panther sitting on my couch. I felt there should have been a golden collar around his neck; his full, shoulder-length brown hair a salon-tended mane. 'Some female higher being keeps him as her precious pet', I thought, seating myself beside him and wishing again that I hadn't worn a black mini skirt which revealed entirely too much of my slender thighs to his predator's eyes.

"You look like you always get what you want," I declared impulsively, reaching for the wine bottle, but he intercepted me, refilling my glass and handing it to me without smiling, as if red wine was a miracle one should seriously appreciate.

"That's very perceptive of you!" Steve said, laughing. "His parents are filthy rich; he's never worked a day in his life. And that's why he's our new singer, because he's putting loads of money into the band." He was kidding of course, but not really. That was the amazing thing about Steve; he had absolutely no tact, but he could get away with it like a five-year-old remains innocently cute no matter what he says or does.

"He's an awesome singer." Jackie lit a cigarette. "And you'd love his lyrics; they're as out there as your poems."

"You write poetry?" Ray asked me.

"Sort of," I replied modestly.

"And boy, are they out there!" My roommate repeated. "Why don't you show some to him?"

"Not now."

"Why not?"

"Because…"

"Maybe some other time." Ray rescued me.

I smiled at him appreciatively. I was attracted to him; there was no question about it. He had a classically handsome face, and the tipsier I got, the more it looked like an ancient statue come to life. Yet there was also a firm, modern edge to his features that gave the sensitive depth of his expression an intense, penetrating power; the carved beauty of his lips enhanced by the fact that he never smiled and barely moved them when he spoke, very quietly. 'He's hypnotizing me', I thought. 'The way he just looks at me, so steadily, so seriously, and I can't concentrate because all I can think about is how to get him to smile. Yet why hasn't he mentioned my dreaming with Alex? Because, he's probably smart enough to know it's a very touchy subject… Oh, Christ, I forgot to listen to what he was saying'…

"Don't you think so, Isabel?" His delicious cupid's mouth looked as if it was waiting for the invisible kiss of my appreciation.

"I'm afraid I don't know anything at this moment, I've had a little too much wine."

He smiled.

"Finally!" I exclaimed.

"Finally what?"

"You finally smiled."

"Oh. So you like happy people."

"I didn't say that…"

He smiled again. "I knew you'd be upset if I said that."

It was then that I realized I was dealing with a fully conscious human being. "I'm sorry." I apologized for the way I had labeled him in my mind. Then suddenly Steve and Jackie got up and I felt like strangling her with her own stupid grin as they left the room.

"I wonder where they're going?" Ray's expression was so convincingly curious and innocent that I started laughing despite the fact that I hated the situation. Yet nothing mattered, not really, because Alex wasn't waiting for me in dreams anymore. I sighed, and instantly regretted it; now he probably thought I was anxious to follow their example.

"God only knows," I replied, not meeting his eyes but unable to avoid the vision of his chest where his white shirt fell open.

"I don't think He wants to know," he said, sensing, and very cleverly handling, my paranoid state.

"No, he probably doesn't," I agreed, smiling shyly while noticing his lean hips and long legs as he fell comfortably back on the couch while giving me that content sideways glance that made him look like a goddess' pet. And suddenly I felt like telling him everything I was thinking. Why not? I had nothing to lose and everything to gain, maybe. "You're a big feline," I began, and he just kept staring at me, but I could feel he was into it; the conscious warmth of his soul rubbing against mine like a cat that wants to be pet. "I can almost see the golden leash of the goddess who owns you around your neck." His eyes widened slightly, unable to believe what I was saying but wanting me to go on. "You're lucky she loves you so much she lets you go anywhere and do anything you like, but she has her eye on you..." I glanced beyond him at the window and the fact that he quickly looked over his shoulder excited me so much I thought, 'Maybe he *is* the answer to all my problems. It seems like he's willing to play, and get into it'.

"Go on," he urged quietly, fingering the stem of his empty glass.

"You're into the whole idea of magic and power, aren't you?" He didn't say anything, which clearly meant he was. "Well, I have to warn you that curiosity killed the cat, and that's all you are, a playful, curious little kitten no matter how much you think you know."

"Really?"

'Oh, good, he's getting angry'… "Yes, really. All you know is this little ball called the earth and you're idly playing with the indestructible string of energy behind everything, but its hopelessly tangled by ignorance and a selfish lust for power, which makes it seem so complicated and intricately grand when it is really very simple."

"And I suppose you know what the great secret is?"

"Yes, Love, and the unending creativity contained within it. That's the only power there is, the only natural or supernatural force, no matter how many names physical and spiritual sciences give it. The truth is that the only occult dimension is your own heart, so you'd better know it well and devote your life to its growth, else you might not like what you see and experience when you die."

"Uh-huh." He leaned forward slowly and set his glass down on the coffee table.

'Now he's going to tell me I'm weird and have no right to speak to him like this'…

"You seem to know me very well, Isabel. Is it possible we've been dreaming together and I, quite stupidly and unfortunately, don't remember?"

I laughed, more pleased by his reaction than I cared to admit. "No, we haven't, but we could try it." Then I felt like a whore, betraying Alex and my love for him by offering the open space of my psyche up like my sex to a stranger; the sensuality of my imagination like my flesh.

"Could we?"

His quiet voice, the positive yet maturely subdued way in which he was reacting, made me think angrily, 'Why should I feel guilty about trying to forget Alex? It's what he wants. It's what's right. He's married and wants to dream with his wife, so I have to try and find my own fulfillment somehow'. "Yes," I answered just as quietly.

He grasped my hand, gazing at me intently. I didn't say anything, so he pulled me to him.

* * *

I was with Ray in my bedroom and part of me couldn't believe it. I was tired. At first his experienced positioning of my submissive body had been so consuming that I couldn't feel sad because I was too busy accommodating his energetic motion against me, inside me, all around me.

"I like your speakers," he declared, pulling his long, slender dick out of me and yanking me up off the bed in one motion. "Let's be the music!" My speakers are quite tall and sturdy, and he made me bend over one of them by putting his hand on the back of my neck and gently but inexorably imposing his will on me. I was beginning to find his demanding virility a bit tiring, in more ways than one. I felt like a soulless rag doll listening to him moan as he penetrated me from behind, and I experienced the sensation of his thrusts in a strangely detached fashion, as if my soul was hovering somewhere just above my body watching action that should have been exciting, but wasn't. I had no profound sense of self left; I was only a physical void temporarily being filled by a dick that opened my pussy up around it, the sadness in my chest growing tighter and hotter than my sex the longer and the harder he fucked me.

"Ray, stop, please…"

He pulled out of me reluctantly and helped me straighten up. "Have you had enough?" he asked smugly.

I sighed, falling into his arms to enjoy his tender embrace and the illusion of love it provided.

"I love your hair," he whispered. "It could strangle me all by itself.'

"You're as morbid as I am." It was a compliment.

"You're not morbid." He was feeling me all over slowly.

"Jackie says I am."

"She's just stupid."

"That's not very nice, Ray."

"I never said I was nice."

"You're not, you don't seem to want to come until there's nothing left of me."

"That's right, I want you to dissolve in my arms and leave only the web of your hair wrapped around me and your teeth buried in my neck."

I laughed.

"I want to dream with you, Isabel."

My heart suddenly felt like a luscious chunk of meat he was hungry for, and I almost wished he would rip it out of my chest right then and there and put me out of my misery. Without my dreams of Alex, life was an intolerably boring cell. I had always hated seeing wild lions and tigers in cages at the zoo, their powerful muscles growing depressingly lax, and that was how my soul was beginning to feel lapping up the food and water of day-to-day circumstances and experiences, but wasting away without the lush, divinely free space my love for Alex opened up.

I got under the covers to indicate I was tired, and joining me beneath them, Ray wrapped his arms and legs around me like a boa, his selfish possessiveness just barely disguised as considerate tenderness. "Oh, Ray, I'm so miserable," I confessed.

"Baby, don't be!" he breathed, kissing me gently, as if my tongue was an invalid his was gradually nursing beck to health. "Don't be..." He kept slowly caressing me, fondling my breasts with one hand while lightly teasing my clitoris with the ball of his thumb, and I began suffering the illusion that I wanted him again; the penetration of his understanding momentarily soothed the existential void left inside me by my impossible love for Alex.

"Finish taking me," I whispered. "I want to feel you come inside me."

He rolled on top of me and obligingly plunged his hard-on back into my desperately clinging hole.

My body began inexorably climaxing as he rubbed himself against me, both selfishly and generously stimulating my G-spot with the head of his erection as my cunt clamped possessively around his full rigid length. Yet even as a small, reluctant orgasm tickled my pelvis, I was sinking deeper and deeper into despair. 'Oh, Alex, I love you! I can't forgot you'!

Ray's face above me was strangely blank, his individuality mysteriously eroded by pleasure. It was so different from the way Alex's face contorted with a passionate distinction when he was coming, like a perfectly cut diamond... I couldn't pretend anymore that I was trying to forget him; it was impossible, even with another handsome man's cum drenching my insides.

* * *

I opened my eyes and peace flooded me. White light flowed into waves and gradually dimmed, the brightness concentrated into a glimmering foam breaking gently for as far as I could see. I wasn't even conscious of a shore until I thought about it, then I felt, and saw, the fine white sand I had experienced in my first dream with Alex. I breathed deeply, relieved not to feel Ray's arms around me. I was free; I was inside Alex's eyes, the luminous blue of the sky and the sea alive with the passion and beauty of his inner vision. I gazed out at the horizon and saw Alex's face appearing. From the undulation of the water his mouth took form. Then the pale expanse of his cheekbones were formed by rays of light creating his face, the luminous cloudbank of his brow filled with the charged particles of his thoughts and the lightning bolts of his desire. The wind was his breath, his nose perfectly structured, its two hills sloping into the world of his cheeks, and its central path leading up into his mind and the spirit behind its own manifestation. Then I saw his eyes, the living consciousness of the sky, his pupils windows into the dark universe alive with the eternal, dimensionless reality of Being... the atmosphere was the flesh of his soul, the sand and shore the skin of his body, the grains running through my fingers all his lives in the palm of my dream hand leading to this perfect form of his in the sky.

"I love you, Alex," I stated quietly as seagulls cried it out joyously. I didn't want to wake up and find myself in Ray's arms. I wanted to remain on this peaceful inner shore forever, gazing at the divine structure of Alex's face. And as I sat there without a care in the world, imaginary or real, the sun rose higher in the sky, growing brighter and sending down soft golden rays my soul took joy in caressing like my hand stroking his hair... until a flaming red scorpion suddenly crawled quickly out of the sea towards me...

"Good morning." Ray smiled into my eyes.

"No!" I moaned, turning away from him and clutching my pillow.

"My, that's not very nice." He bent over me, forcing one of his knees between my legs. "Good morning," he repeated firmly.

"Good morning." I closed my eyes.

"Why won't you let me dream with you, Isabel, I want to..."

"Never!" I couldn't control my vehemence even though I didn't want to hurt him, but the fact that he had entered my body didn't give him access to my soul.

"Never, hmm? I'll make you change your mind," he promised quietly.

"No, Ray, I don't think so." I sighed hopelessly.

* * *

"Man, Isabel, I don't believe you!' Jackie shook her head. "What the hell are you anyway, a vampire? You suck guys dry in one night and toss them away. I can't believe you!" But she couldn't help being a little impressed, too. "Steve's freaked out. Those are his two best friends you treated like shit."

"I know. I'm sorry. It won't happen again."

"You bet it won't. Do you think I'm going to keep supplying you with victims? Dreaming with Alex went to your head. You've become completely unrealistic and impossible to live with... so I'm moving in with Steve... we talked about it last night."

"Oh... I'm sorry... it'll definitely be better for you, though, because I have mo intention of changing for anyone." Since my experience with

Ray, there was a hard edge to my personality; I was no longer sympathetic to Jackie's attitude because I had realized that my magical perspective was fragile as a flower, so it was foolish of me to feel condescendingly invulnerable to her scorching cynicism and the perpetual frost of her reason. I was fighting a battle, and since Alex, and what I felt for him, were my prize, in this world or the next, in one form or another, it was all claws out.

"You're a cold bitch, Isabel. You don't care about anyone but yourself and your precious rock star who isn't even real."

"Uh-huh." I retired to my room. I had already decided that even though it was going to be a financial strain, I wasn't getting another roommate. 'I would rather pinch pennies than deal with noxious vibes in my own home. I'll get a cat who'll understand me'.

* * *

I woke up suddenly feeling the warm light of the candle flame on my eyelids flickering as if under a breeze. I lay there unusually content, until I remembered I couldn't have lit a candle before falling asleep because I didn't have any, and besides, all my windows were closed because it was the dead of winter.

I opened my eyes. Yes, I was in my room, but there was someone there with me... I stopped breathing, absolutely terrified to see a man standing beside my speaker... petting Wolfy... and my confused fear swiftly unwound into a limp joy.

I couldn't sit up, but it didn't matter because I knew the darkness around me was his pupils and that it was his vision I was a living part of, so there was nothing to fear. He approached the bed dressed in the suit he had worn at the concert.

"Alex…?"

He sat on the edge of the mattress and stared down at me, not saying anything, not smiling, and my physical paralysis spread to my mind. I had wanted to ask him about the tropical breeze, and if we were really dreaming together again or if I was alone in my own head, but my awareness relaxed so blissfully in his presence I couldn't hold onto thoughts or grasp the significance of any questions. He was here and that was all that was real and mattered.

"Alex… did you miss me?"

"Yes."

'I know why I can't sit up, because he's not smiling', I thought. My body was lying straight and still as his lips, literally the reflection of his mood. "Don't look so serious, Alex, please, it's paralyzing me…"

"I'm sorry."

"Oh, no!" My eyes closed from the weight of his concern.

"Isabel, don't wake up." He shook me gently.

"No, I don't want to…" I was able to sit up now. "But I'm in *your* dream this time, Alex, and you really have to want me here."

He just stared at me again so I grasped one of his hands desperately, a blessed island in the darkness full of the currents of his doubts and fears; visibly menacing shadows around the warm heart of the dream that was the candle burning between us.

"I love you, Alex, and it's not a silly crush, or an unrealistic infatuation, or an adolescent dream, or an idealistic fantasy, or anything else it can be labeled because I don't expect anything from it except the feeling itself… I mean, I know you're a mortal man whose married and has his own life and no time to spare, really, because you're so busy being creative… but that's all I want you to do is keep being yourself, because

I feel the beauty of life and the mystery of the universe through you, and that's what I want, that's what's important to me, for you to keep helping me sustain my dreams with your spirit, that's all... although I guess that's a lot...

"That's all you want from me?" He smiled.

'Well... I cannot tell a lie..."

"How are you, Isabel?" He squeezed my hand affectionately.

"I'm fine, I guess. Why are you dressed up, Alex, it's the middle of the night?" I curled up like an embryo to rest my cheek in his hand.

"I thought I had experienced just about everything until you made me start being conscious in my dreams. They were always fantastic, but now I can remember them clearly, and having a say in them is certainly interesting."

"I'm so glad you're into it."

"I don't know... it kind of spoils you..."

I looked at him again. "I wish I was a goddess so I could spoil you even more!"

"And what about you?" He was very serious. "You need someone who can be with you in real life and take care of you, someone to spoil you too, Isabel. You're very beautiful and very special; you shouldn't waste yourself by just dreaming with me."

"Oh, God, no one else turns me on, not at all. They just don't have your spirit... you know I'm special, so I need a special man..."

"There are a lot of intense people out there you simply don't know about yet, Isabel."

"And I have to try and find them, right?" I asked dryly.

"You have to be open to the possibility, Isabel," he repeated my name tenderly, "you could make a man very happy."

I fell back across the bed. "I'd do anything to get you out of my head, Alex, but the truth of the matter is no one gives me the power to dream the way you do."

"I told you, Isabel, you just haven't met him yet."

"But what if I insist on believing that you're the only man for me? It doesn't put me in a tower, I still meet people and men, yet all they do is confirm my belief that I'm a sacred part of you... I want to be your priestess... I want to help nurture your inner life's muscles, which you're just beginning to flex by conscious dreaming like a baby curiously studies the magic of his hand in the crib, not really able to control it yet... but unlike a baby, you're aware of your growing inner dimensions, your expanding power... physical laws are your own limbs, Alex, and I just want to be able to talk to you about these things every now and then in dreams... I don't want you to fly home to me; I want to meet you in the sky, because one day you might need me... I'm sorry. I know I talk too much. I blab on and on. You're right; I have to be open to the possibility of meeting someone else so my thoughts aren't constantly wrapped around you like a spider's web, using you to nourish my own supernatural kinkiness..."

He put a finger to my lips, silencing me and reminding me of the straight feather worn by the ancient Egyptian goddess of truth. He stared at me, absorbing what I had said as much as a he cared to, like someone invited to a sumptuous banquet is not obliged to partake of anything but what he desires, my ideas a dancing girl twirling around him tossing flowers into his lap. But if they hit him blatantly in the face, no matter how beautiful they were, they became obnoxious; I was worried I had said too much too fast.

"I came tonight to apologize for killing you." His hand caressed my cheek briefly, like the wing of a bird communicating to me all the bliss of heaven.

"That's all right, you can do it anytime." I gazed at him longingly as Wolfy's purring dream-body jumped onto the bed.

"What's his name?"

"Lord Wolfson, but I call him Wolfy."

"Isabel…"

"Yes?" I held my breath.

"I think I have to wake up now."

My heart deflated like a red balloon after nearly touching the roof of heaven, my mind spiraling wildly down to the harsh ground of reality as I desperately tried to think of something that might get him to stay a little longer. "Alex…" He was silent again, avoiding my eyes. "I love you, that's all." I closed my eyes in despair. He moved, and I braced myself for his absence, but then I suddenly felt his lips on mine, ironically like the prince kissing Sleeping Beauty, because what I dreaded more than anything was waking up and losing him. I mustered all my willpower and reached up for him.

"I have to go," he whispered, yet he let my arms twine around him and draw him slowly down into a deep kiss, our tongues twisting together like the roots of our rapidly growing need for each other.

"I worship you, Alex, please let me give you everything," I begged him quietly, and he flung the bed sheet off me. The candle flame flickered dangerously in the gust of air. I watched it, terrified, until it steadied, but then my awareness flickered as my pulse accelerated when he suddenly stood up and began undressing. I couldn't think; I was utterly consumed by the experience of watching his naked flesh emerge like moonlight from the darkness of his suit.

* * *

"Meow!"

"Wolfy! Did you miss me, baby?"

"Purr... Purr... Purr..."

RING.

"Hell."

"Purr... Purr..."

RING.

"Hello?"

"Hi, Isabel, it's Jackie."

"Hi, Jackie. How are you?"

"Not so good."

"Why, what's wrong?"

"Steve and I broke up."

"Oh, no…"

"And now I have to look for another place to live…"

"Drag…"

Silence.

"What happened?" I ignored the obvious reason for her call.

"Nothing, really, we both just decided it was time for us to move on. It's natural. I'm not upset about it. It's time to look for adventure; if you get too rooted everything becomes a bore."

"Hmm."

"How's it going with you?"

"Good… I bought a cat."

"Really? Don't tell me, he's black, right?"

"You're so smart."

"Have you gotten another roommate?"

"No, and I'm not going to."

"Why not?"

"Because, I'm into living alone with a cat."

Silence.

"Are you still obsessed with Alex?" she finally asked.

"Yes... I dream with him almost every night again now."

"Oh, Isabel, grow up!"

I hung up.

'I *have* grown up, Jackie, I don't deal with idiots like you anymore. It's amazing how people, in the face of glaring proof, will still stick by their rigid Victorian perceptions of reality. *You* grow up, this is the age of curved time and space and of energy that cannot be created or destroyed, only change its form. "Get it, you idiot?"

* * *

I was having dinner alone as usual, with Wolfy sitting companionably by his own plate, when the doorbell rang. I almost choked on the thought that it was Jackie, but then realized it was unlikely, and curiously buzzed the person in.

"Delivery for Isabel!'

"That's me, the third floor." I gazed down the stairwell and saw what looked like the Garden of Eden ascending towards me, rustling with the motion of the courier completely hidden beneath it. He reached my landing, and I backed away into my apartment more stunned than if the gates of Paradise had suddenly opened before me.

"Beautiful, isn't it?" I saw the bloom of his grin inside the lush foliage. "Somebody really likes you."

"Yes… come in, you can set it there on the floor…" I directed him to the center of my bedroom. "Thanks."

"Sure thing." He left, and I stood at the entrance to my bedroom feeling as if a huge seed had just exploded beneath the wooden boards, germinating in the blink of an eye and magically containing all the variety of flowers on earth. I approached the almost obscene explosion of blossoms, and amidst the leaves saw a small violet card secretly placed. I extracted it carefully. "Oh, Alex!" I collapsed onto my bed, and holding my breath, opened it.

To my dream girl, Isabel,
I love you
And one day, we'll never wake up.

Wolfy rubbed his face against my knee and I caressed him, part of me sadly subdued because I knew this meant Alex and I would never actually be together, yet another part of me, the deepest, truest part of me, was infinitely excited and radiantly happy.

"Meow?" He was asking for permission to go smell the flowers, which I knew he was fond of eating.

"Yes, baby, go ahead." I smiled, setting Alex's card on my night table beside our violet candle.

THE END

Magic Carpet Books Announces its new Paranormal Erotic Romance line

DARK FANTASY

Read an excerpt from the

The Shifting Heart
A Paranormal Erotic
Romance

by Bryn Colvin

England, the Fens, a moody and mysterious land by the sea one-hundred years ago…

Coming back from taking clothes and food to one of the poorer families in the parish, Megan, the vicar's daughter, and Ivy, a servant in the household, are caught in a sudden storm. Soon the flat land is blanketed in snow, leaving the young women unable to find the road; they can no longer even see the spire of Megan's father's church. A tumble into a dyke leaves Megan soaked and half frozen. Ivy is about to leave her to go and find help when suddenly two strikingly handsome men appear as if from nowhere and help the young women back to their cottage, where they are obliged to forget propriety and spend the night.

Megan is enchanted by Jonathan, and finds excuses to visit him, embroiling Ivy in her intrigues. Although Ivy tries to protect her mistress' reputation, she soon becomes the accomplice to an intense love affair. She and Ben, Jonathan's younger brother, strive to protect the lovers, and a gentler bond forms between them.

What Megan does not realize is that the man she has lost her heart to is a Shapeshifter. Jonathan is a wild creature at heart belonging to a hidden world of myth and magic Megan can hardly believe or understand. Yet it is already too late, heart and soul she is possessed by a man who haunts her nights with a passion that begins blurring the line between dreams and reality, a dangerous position indeed for a vicar's daughter…

Turn the page for an exciting excerpt…

Megan

Attendance at the school was very poor the week the snow finally melted. Most of the fields were flooded and, although the roads were passable, many of the children were ill with influenza. Megan considered the absent ones with a heavy heart. It was very likely some of them would never return to her sewing classes; the winters often claimed a child or two. Living in such large families, with ten or twelve of people cramped into tiny cottages and no money to pay for proper food or medicine, they were terribly vulnerable. Her father did what he could, but the battle against abject poverty seemed to be one they could never win.

There were so few girls present that she dismissed them early, knowing their return would be helpful to overstretched mothers. Finding she had a little time on her hands, Megan slipped into the church. It was an ancient building, built when the wool trade was at its height and money flowed through the district. Those days of prosperity were more than a century gone, but the church remained, beautiful and tranquil in spite of everything.

Sitting in one of the pews she gazed up at the ceiling, considering the bosses, with their ornate foliage, before turning her eyes to the altar and the stained glass window behind it. Hands clasped as though in prayer, she whispered into the otherwise silent and empty space. "Help me to do more, and to be strong. Please bless me with the courage to do what I can, and the forbearance to accept when I can do nothing. I do not understand why there has to be so much suffering in this world." It was a thought that had been increasingly on her mind of late as she paid her visits to the poorest among the congregation and tried to find the means to help them.

Her reverie was broken abruptly, although Megan could not have said what disturbed her. Straining her ears, she could discern no change within the small church. Still, her skin crawled and her shoulders prickled as though fingers were teasing against her back. The slight creak of the pew behind her proved finally that she was not alone, but it would be unthinkable to turn around.

Bare fingers brushed against the back of her neck, finding the tiny area of exposed flesh between the collar of her coat and her hair. She shivered and closed her *eyes*. No one should touch her in that way. It was too *intimate*. She hardly dared breathe feeling the rough fingertips glide back and forth over her skin, slipping around her slender throat and then up over her chin to brush lightly against her lips. Megan was trembling, her being fluttering like a leaf in a Fen blow, powerless and in danger of being torn from its rightful place. Moving under a compulsion that she barely understood, she caught those wandering fingers with her own hand. The fingers she had captured were long and slender, the palm narrow, the back dotted with soft, dark hairs – a delicate hand but a male one, with dirt under the nails. The shirt cuff was worn and threadbare in places, the jacket too short in the arm. Each tiny detail absorbed her, a revelation in its own right as his fingers tangled with hers, arousing a sensitivity she had not known her hands possessed.

"Beauty," a voice whispered low, caressing her ears with its passionate tone.

She sighed.

"I know you!" he said, and the words sounded like recognition of her soul, not a mere acknowledgement of acquaintance.

She dared to turn her head, slowly.

Eyes of the darkest blue she had ever seen returned her gaze. She stared at him openly, meeting his intense stare with her own searching scrutiny. He had sought her out; there could be no other explanation.

"Seth," she whispered his name into the echoing church.

He nodded. "You?"

"Megan West."

"Megan..." he tried the name, almost as though he was tasting it. In his mouth it sounded musical and exotic. His long fingers stroked along her wrist, sliding easily under her sleeve to the tender skin of her forearm, his soul-divining gaze never leaving her face. "Do you know... that tumbledown place... over the way?" He spoke awkwardly, as though having to think carefully about every word.

"Do you mean the old abbey ruins not far from the road to Norsey?"

He considered this for a moment. "Looks like stone trees."

"That would be the abbey," she said, wondering how on earth he could fail to know so simple and obvious a thing.

"I'll be there in the afternoon," he said, "tomorrow... any afternoon. I'll be there."

She realized what he meant, the implied invitation in his words. He smiled, and she found herself nodding.

Once he had gone, she stared into the space of the church, searching her soul. She should have resisted his advances and protested against those uninvited, improper caresses. She should never have suggested she might meet with him in that lonely *place*. It was not right or *appropriate*, she thought. It was not what she, as the daughter of a vicar and an upstanding member of society, should be doing. He could hardly ask for her hand in marriage. His intentions therefore must be less than honorable, whatever that actually meant. Megan had been taught to guard her honor without having any real idea what it might need guarding from. Even though he had gone, it still felt as though he was touching her. The skin he had tantalized with questing fingertips still hummed, making her acutely aware of the way in which she had been explored. It had been a fleeting thing but, now that he was gone, she hankered after more.

* * *

Lying had proved all too easy. It was almost true for Megan to say she wanted to go walking, to look for the violets and primroses where they peeked out beneath the hedges. Her father was teaching, as he often did in the afternoons. Her mother had undertaken to visit an elderly neighbor, and agreed that a little fresh air would do the girl a great deal of good. It had been a long time since Megan had intentionally spoken falsely to her parents. It gave her the most terrible, powerful, unfettered feeling. By the time she set out along the road she was shocked by what she had done and half afraid of what might yet happen. It hardly seemed as though she was doing these things herself. Yet how else could it be? She was walking out to an assignation with a young man, having willfully misled her parents on the matter. Megan knew she was longer their docile child and that she was breaking all sorts of unspoken rules.

The road to Norsey was higher than the surrounding fields. Where sometimes cattle grazed or heavy horses pulled their ploughs, birds now skittered across recently formed lakes. In a few days the melt water would be gone and those many folk who survived by tilling the land would be back at their labors. With the fields flooded, there was no one much about. The abbey ruins loomed on the horizon, visible for a long time before she drew near them. They looked foreboding, dark shadows against the pale sun of early spring. Megan wondered what she would do when she reached that spot – if she would climb down from the road and walk amongst the remains of ancient piety or turn back for the safety of home. The thought of Seth's brooding expression and the touch of his fingers on her neck drew her onwards.

Grass grew bright and luscious where the feet of penitents passed in years gone by. Pillars that had once supported a great arching roof now stood alone or lay where they had fallen. They were indeed like great stone trees, she realized. The place was still and empty. Above her the vast expanse of blue stretched to the ends of the world. There might be no people to see her, but there was no secrecy under so open a sky. The abbey stood a little way above the water, connected to the roadway by a broad swathe of muddy ground. Aside from the ducks bobbing on the flood there were no signs of life at all...

Movement at the periphery of her vision caught her attention. She turned. For a moment, she thought there was someone standing in the shadow of a crumbling wall watching her. She had the impression of a pale face and long, loose hair. The wind caught at the overhanging ivy, turning it, and the illusion of a woman melted away. Megan laughed at her own guilty nervousness and at the tricks her untamed imagination could play upon her.

Having assured herself she was quite alone, she walked down towards the water, being careful on the slippery ground. It crossed her mind he might have been teasing her, and the possibility saddened her somewhat. He might never have meant to meet with her; this might be some cruel jest at her expense.

A dark ripple of movement caught her eye. Bubbles trailed on the shimmering surface, rising through liquid so muddy it almost looked black. A dark spot broke through the flood-water, and the shiny head of an otter emerged. Amazed to see one of these creatures again so soon after her previous sighting, Megan watched in fascination. If nothing else, this would give her something to share with her father. Water slid from the animal's thick pelt as it confidently approached, its body undulating as it moved. It paused a few feet away from her, keen little eyes turned in her direction, whiskers twitching. She half expected it to turn and run, but it remained.

She squeezed her eyes tightly shut, opened them, and blinked again. It seemed to Megan that her eyes were playing tricks on her. The otter looked bigger somehow than it had on first emerging. As she watched in utter disbelief, the lithe creature shimmered and shook. With every breath she took, the thing she saw looked less like an otter. With her heart drumming a wild tattoo and her stomach lurching, she backed away until she felt cold stone behind her and could retreat no further. The Lord's Prayer was on her lips, chanted instinctively as the only defense she could reach for, but all it served to do was calm her terror a little as the insanity before her continued. Where there had been fur now there was naked flesh, lean and muscular in the sunlight. She could not have said which shocked her most – the impossible transformation she had witnessed, or the vision of nude masculinity that now stood before her. Paralyzed like some prey that knows it cannot escape the fox, Megan could only stare open mouthed at the man who appeared before her.

Seth's dark hair still sparkled with drops of water. His narrow face showed no traces of otter features, and his long limbs looked human enough. Megan knew she ought not to look, but her gaze was drawn down from his compelling eyes to the breadth of his shoulders and the bare skin of his chest. Then further did she dare to examine, skimming over his smooth, flat stomach to the rod that stood out from between his thighs. She had no idea what it was even as somewhere deep within her, something primal and hungry stirred. Her mind might have been kept innocent of men, but her body understood.

He strode over the grass towards her, his domination of the situation absolute. It seemed to Megan he was king of the moment, ruler of the soil beneath his feet, of the beautiful afternoon, and her own delicate body. There was no escaping his hands as he sough her breasts and hips. His mouth covered hers and she surrendered to his tongue, letting him penetrate between her lips to steal away her reason. Crushed against the wall, she was overwhelmed. All of her upbringing screamed out against such wild, improper behavior, but her body was his co-conspirator, responding to his questing hands as buttons were pulled open and cloth dispensed with. He pushed her jacket from her shoulders, opened her blouse, and pressed kisses onto her bare shoulders. Somehow his fingers found their way down the front of her stays, teasing at her small breasts until she was giddy from sensation.

"I should not..." she began, but his mouth closed over hers again, stifling the protest.

He stepped away, fixing her with his smoldering gaze. Megan realized her breasts were heaving and that she could barely breathe. She hardly knew what was happening to her. Reaching for his hand, she drew it to her lips and kissed each fingertip in turn.

"I want you," he said simply.

The words sent a thrill through her even though she could not fully grasp their significance.

"What do you want me for?" she asked innocently.

"I want to touch your body."

She flushed scarlet at this, but he had not finished.

"I want your skin against mine," he continued.

A deep yearning inside her rose up at this.

"Let me lie with you." He stepped closer, pulling up her skirts. She felt his fingers between her thighs, caressing her through her undergarments. The sensation shocked her and filled her with fear. This seemed wrong, and right, all at once. She craved more of it, but begged him to stop. Those long and lethal fingers of his were at play, skillfully mastering the mysteries of her clothing.

"No," she whispered.

He laid her down in the sodden grass, pulling her clothing away so her bare skin was upon the peaty earth. She tried to cover herself with her hands, but he pulled them away also, placing his mouth on her breasts and then her thighs, kissing the places she had been ashamed to show him. His fingers explored the dark triangle of her hair between her legs, prizing her open and exploring her virgin cleft. It was an uncomfortable, troubling feeling.

"Please…" She hardly knew if she wanted him to stop or continue. He took her words as encouragement, working his fingers deeper inside her.

"You've not had a man before," he observed.

"No!" she breathed.

Their eyes met, and her fear melted in the face of his desire. He pushed a little harder. His lips closed over each of her delicate nipples in turn, tasting them to the full. She reached for him then, finding the courage to touch his chest and arms. In response he smiled at her, a sweet reward for her daring. She continued, exploring the small protrusions of his nipples and wondering if she dared to touch that curious manifestation between his legs.

Some strange alchemy had been worked upon her body. The discomfort melted away, leaving a sweet sensation in its stead. She lay still, gazing up into his face, compelled by the hunger in his eyes to surrender as he worked some of his magic upon her.

"Don't fight it," he commanded.

She trembled, gasped, and wriggled beneath his hands.

"That's it," he said.

He moved onto her, resting his weight on his elbows and looking down into her face. The shock of his cock piercing her was startling indeed. She gasped, not knowing if what she felt was pain or pleasure. He rocked slowly upon her, filling her body with shivering, tremulous feelings and painful delight as he possessed her.

When it was done, he slipped hurriedly from her. There were no soft words or explanations. He sauntered down over the muddy grass and plunged into the water, vanishing beneath the surface with barely a sound.

The Shifting Heart

Shocked and ashamed by what she had done, Megan dressed rapidly. There was blood on her thighs, the traces of her deflowering showing crimson on her skin. Grabbing a handful of grass, she tried to wipe it away, but it was drying already. She pulled on her dress, covering the mud on her back and the stains on her body. The water was still, the afternoon tranquil once *more*. Surely, it could not have *happened*? She must have dreamed it all, so impossible did the afternoon seem. When she rose and walked, there was a profound ache in her loins. He could not have come to her wearing the skin of an otter and seduced her body so utterly. She could hardly believe she had lost her honor so quickly. She understood now what the words from the wedding service meant – man and woman joined as one *flesh*. It is not so simple as that, surely? She must have dreamed it.

Megan knew she was no longer pure or good, that she had transgressed and tasted the forbidden fruits of pleasure. She could hardly think, but tidied herself as best she could and stumbled home. There was no doubt at all in her mind that she would go back to the ruins as soon as she could to see if it had been but a moment's madness...

Ivy

On the first sunny day for over a week, Ivy set about her washing with grim determination. On waking, she could smell the change in the air and knew there was some chance the weather might last long enough for drying. It could well be her last chance before the Spring to launder their bedding and get it aired, and she was determined to make the best of it. As was often the case, Ben had been out since first light. He had found a few days work on one of the small farms, which would bring in much needed money. Her arms ached as she stretched to pin up the damp washing. Still, it pleased her to see it flapping in the breeze.

Out of nowhere came the warm press of a man's body behind her, and hands that wandered confidently over her stomach and breasts. She smiled, closing her eyes wondering what Ben was doing back so soon. His questing fingers found her nipples, rubbing at them through her layers of clothing. It was pure delight to be touched in this way and she felt herself melting into desire. She wriggled against him suggestively and reached her hands back to return the caresses. The feel of bare skin sent the first warning signals through her mind, but her body was enraptured and aroused, making it difficult to concentrate on anything aside from pleasure.

Wordlessly, he pushed her down onto her knees and, with his hand flat on her back, pressed her towards the ground. While they often played and flirted outside the house, Ben had never sought to take her in daylight in so public a place. Something was wrong. Ivy felt a trickle of uncertainty pass through her. Glancing back over her shoulder, she saw someone who looked a lot like her husband, so much so that for a moment she half believed it was him. She could only see his shoulder and his hair. Little of his face was visible aside from one high cheekbone and the angular jut of his jaw. His hands were on her thighs, lifting her skirts and exploring her under garments. She could not see him well enough to be sure. Her mind and heart raced each other as fear and arousal competed for domination. She wanted to be taken, her body ached for it, but her alarm was growing with very moment. Ben's touch was not as rough as this.

Ivy knew she should cry out or try to resist because the strong hands that ripped away her undergarments were not her husband's. This was not Ben's way with her; he was always gentle and careful. Her seducer's fingers found her slickness, exploring the depths of her hungry sex with practiced ease. He delved into her and she did not fight him, succumbing to the pleasure he was giving her. When his hand withdrew, she knew what was coming next.

"Don't," she said weakly, but it was a protest she barely meant, and her voice was so low he might not even have heard her.

His cock drove into her, hard and insistent. Fingers dug into her hips. Everything about him was fierce and urgent. She could feel her nipples aching in their stays. Her seducer was relentless, pummeling her softness with a ferocity that left her gasping and shaking. She did not know what to do and so she did nothing, letting him make free with her. Her breath came in shuddering gasps as she pushed her fingers into the soft grass beneath her. Anyone could see her here. Anyone could find them, including Ben, and yet the perilous nature of her situation only seemed to ignite her further. Sex with her husband was sweet, but this was wildly erotic, turning her on in ways she had not known were possible.

The strength of her reactions was as startling as his ferocious possession of her body. She came as she had never come before, the climax shaking her to the very core of her being. His grip on her grew tighter, his strokes more persistent, his hips thrusting faster and harder until at last she felt the earth shattering eruption of his sex deep within hers.

When he finally let her go, Ivy collapsed down across the grass, finding that her knees could no longer support her weight. For a while she could neither think nor move. Blissful exhaustion claimed her. As her wits made their slow return, she realized she must discover the identity of the man who had taken her so utterly. She sat up, feeling bruised from the intensity of his penetrations. Raising her head, she mustered all her courage and looked the man straight in the face.

Kneeling before her, with a smile of wicked indulgence on his handsome face, was Seth. She covered her mouth, realizing the full extent of the transgression, yet her body was trembling from the violent thrill of it and longing for more.

"What you doing here?" he asked casually.

"I married your brother," she said, unable to continue looking him in the eye.

"Humph," he snorted, clearly unimpressed by this news. "Where he be?"

"Working," she answered, "back in the evening, I'd think."

"Then I'll get something for the pot."

His casualness about the whole business was more distressing than anything else, but she was roused from her attack of self-pity by a peculiar feeling on her skin, as though the air around her was prickling with energy. When she risked looking up, the man was gone, and in his place sat a sleek, bright-eyed otter. Her breath caught in her throat and she stared fearfully at the animal before her. Ben always talked about Seth's shifting as though it was something easy and natural. Even having missed the moment of change, the shock of it still overwhelmed her. She thought the otter had the same laughing expression on its face as the man had worn only a few seconds ago.

Low to the ground, the dark-furred creature set off at a rolling gait, vanishing into the long grass. When he was out of sight, she buried her face in her hands. She couldn't cry. Guilt and elation battled within her. Seth had taken her, and it had been a glorious experience. She had betrayed Ben, the dearest, kindest person she had ever *known*. It was not my *fault*, she tried to tell *herself*. Not my fault at *all*. She had not realized her husband's brother was behind her, and once she did find out, it was too late, but in her heart she knew how much she had desired him. Ever since the day when she spied on him in the ruins and watched him take his pleasure with Megan, she had wanted him. There was no denying it, not to herself.

An hour later he was back, his pelt waterlogged and a large trout in his jaws. Ivy set to work on it at once, glad of having something to do with her still trembling hands.

"Him got any clothes spare?"

She supposed he must have changed again. Resisting the temptation to look round and feast her eyes on the splendor of his naked body, she nodded.

"There's some in the box up in the bedroom. It's worn, I was going to use it for patching."

"It'll do."

She heard him pad softly up the stairs and sank her teeth into her lower lip. It was evident Seth meant to stay, and that things were going to be complicated in the extreme.

"Smells like trout," Ben called out cheerily as he stomped the mud off his boots outside the door.

Ivy looked up as he came in, struggling to find a smile and half afraid to look him the eye for fear he would see the guilt in hers. She nodded.

"Where you get trout?" he asked.

She gestured vaguely towards the ladder. "We got a visitor."

His brow furrowed, the look on his face questioning.

"Seth," she said, voicing his name as carefully as she could.

On cue, the young man loped quietly down the stairs. The trousers were almost threadbare and a little too short in the leg for him. He had not bothered to fasten up the shirt, and his muscular chest was very much on display.

Ben laughed with delight and stepped forward to embrace his sibling. "You been gone a long time. Where you been?"

"Here and there," Seth replied dismissively.

"It's good to have you home," Ben said enthusiastically.

"And you got Ivy, and I weren't here," Seth observed. "House looks different."

The Shifting Heart

Ivy had made a rag rug for the living room, and it cheered the little space considerably. She had picked and dried herbs, which now hung from the wall in large bunches. It was not the stark cottage it had been before Seth's departure.

As she washed their few dishes after the meal, she decided it would be best to say nothing about the afternoon. The two brothers were happy in each other's company, talking and laughing together. She had no desire to sow discord between them or to confess her complicity in what had *happened*. It had been a moment's insanity, no *more*. Now that Seth knew she was pledged to Ben, he would surely respect that and leave her alone? Now that she knew he was around, she could guard herself against being led astray. But even as she was telling herself no such thing could ever occur again, part of her mind was revisiting her seduction and reveling in the memory...

Guilty Pleasures by Maria Isabel Pita

Guilty Pleasures explores the passionate willingness of women throughout the ages to offer themselves up to the forces of love. Historical facts are seamlessly woven into intensely graphic sexual encounters.

Beneath the cover of *Guilty Pleasures* you will find intensely erotic love stories with a profound feel for the different centuries and cultures where they take place. An ancient Egyptian princess... a courtesan rising to fame in Athen's Golden Age...a Transylvanian Count's wicked bride... and many more are all one eternal woman in *Guilty Pleasures*.

0-9755331-5-0 **$16.95**

The Collector's Edition of The Lost Erotic Novels
Dr. Major LaCartilie, Editor

The history of erotic literature is long and distinguished. It holds valuable lessons and insights for the general reader, the sociologist, the student of sexual behavior, and the literary specialist interested in knowing how people of different cultures and different times acted and how these actions relate to the present. They are presented to the reader exactly as they first appeared in print by writers who were, in every sense, representative of their time: *The Instruments of the Passion & Misfortunes of Mary*–Anonymous; *White Stains* - Anaïs Nin & Friends; *Innocence* - Harriet Daimler

0-9755331-0-X **$16.95**

The Ties That Bind
by Vanessa Duriés

The incredible confessions of a thrillingly unconventional woman. From the first page, this chronicle of dominance and submission will keep you gasping with its vivid depictions of sensual abandon. At the hand of Masters Georges, Patrick, Pierre and others, this submissive seductress experiences pleasures she never knew existed. Re-print of the French bestseller.

0-9766510-1-7 **$14.95**

Ironwood

James Carrington's bleak prospects were transformed overnight when he was offered a choice position at Ironwood, a unique finishing school where young women were trained to become premiere Ladies of Pleasure.

Ironwood Revisited

In *IRONWOOD REVISITED*, we follow James' rise to power in that garden of erotic delights. We come to understand how Ironwood, with its strict standards and iron discipline has acquired its enviable reputation among the world's most discriminating connoisseurs.

Images of Ironwood

IMAGES OF IRONWOOD presents selected scenes of unrelenting sensuality, of erotic longing, and of those bizarre proclivities which touch the outer fringe of human sexuality.

0-9766510-2-5   **$17.95**

Send check or money order to:

Magic Carpet Books
PO Box 473
New Milford, CT 06776

Postage free in the United States add $2.50 for
packages outside the United States

MagicCarpetBooks@aol.com